Engaging the Boss

NOELLE ADAMS

D1523094

CHAPTER ONE

Sarah Stratford had learned eavesdropping was dangerous when she overheard a neighbor say she was an unattractive child.

At age eleven, she'd been a little chubby with bushy red hair and dead-white skin. Instead of resenting her neighbor for the unkind words, Sarah had cried because she'd known they were true.

Seventeen years later, she knew she shouldn't eavesdrop on her boss's phone conversation. He hadn't closed the door to his office, however, and the only way not to hear was to cover her ears or leave the laboratory.

Sarah did neither. She tried to focus the DNA sequence projected on one of the lab's high-end monitors, but she couldn't help but listen.

Her boss, Jonathan Damon, was on the phone with his corporate-mogul uncle, and she could hear a tense note in his voice. He'd never said a word to her about his notorious family, but she knew he wasn't close to them. She also knew this conversation wasn't a good one.

"I understand the Damon name is important to you. I know you want us to settle down and have kids. But I have plenty of time for that. I'm only thirty-five." Jonathan's tone was overly patient, as if he were reining in his temper. In the three years she'd worked for him, she'd never seen Jonathan express anger. That patient tone was as close as he came.

Sarah didn't like to think of herself as a nosy person, at least not in general. With Jonathan, however, it was different.

If she were ever in the position to give advice to other women, the first thing she would tell them was never fall in love with your boss. It was a hopeless, never-ending form of torture—to have the object of your affection always right there in front of you but never actually be able to claim him.

It also made you want to eavesdrop on his private conversations.

"That was ages ago. I dated her in grad school," Jonathan was saying now. "We haven't talked in years, and there was never any future in that relationship."

Her curiosity piqued again, Sarah glanced toward the office door, but it was half-closed and Jonathan was out of sight.

One of the problems with loving her boss was that even the possibility of a relationship would jeopardize her position. She was proud of the career she'd built for herself so far. She'd completed a PhD in genetics at Stanford and gotten an enviable position in Jonathan's private lab in Iceland, researching the genetics behind multiple sclerosis. She could honestly say she had her dream job, rather than dealing with the commercialization and politics of a pharmaceutical company, which was probably what she'd be doing if she weren't doing this.

And she could lose this dream job if she ever acted on her feelings for Jonathan. His work was everything to him—his entire world—and he wouldn't put up with anything that threatened it, including an assistant who was too distracted by feelings to do her job well.

"That's ridiculous," Jonathan said in that same patient tone. "We're doing really important work here. You can't be threatening to cut us off just because—"

His uncle obviously had interrupted him since he stopped midsentence. Then, "Okay. I understand. I understand. To tell you the truth, there *is* someone. I've been trying to keep it private, but, well, we're actually engaged."

Another pause.

"Yes, engaged to be married."

Another pause.

"Probably in a few months. We haven't set a date."

During the longer silence as Cyrus Damon responded on the other end of the line, Sarah felt like she'd been crushed under a falling weight. The shocked pain at what she'd heard was so powerful she literally couldn't stand up. She found a stool and lowered herself onto it, trying to force her feelings back down where she could control them.

After all, she had no legitimate cause to be upset, even though she'd never known Jonathan was even *in* a relationship. She'd always known she could never have him for herself. He was her boss, and he was off-limits in every way.

Plus even if she hadn't worked for him, he would never want *her*.

When she could move again, she opened the top drawer in her desk and grabbed a peppermint ball. She'd always had a sweet tooth, one that wouldn't go away. When she started working for Jonathan, she'd actually lost ten pounds—not because he was a health nut but because most of the time he forgot about eating. But she couldn't give up all her sweets.

She liked the round, soft, puffed kind of peppermint balls. A couple of years ago, she'd asked her then-boyfriend Matt to pick her up a bag when he was in Reykjavik. He'd mistakenly gotten her the hard, saucer-shaped kind. She'd just smiled and thanked him since she hadn't wanted him to know she was disappointed. But she hated the hard kind.

The following day, the hard ones had disappeared from her drawer and the good ones had taken their place. Now, every time they were getting low, a new bag would miraculously appear.

Just one of the reasons she loved the man she worked for.

Jonathan was still talking on the phone, mostly murmuring, "Yes" and "Of course."

Then he finally said, "Fine. I'll see if she can come." He hung up a few seconds later.

Sarah picked up the silver travel mug Jonathan drank from—inscribed with the words Lab Rat—and carried it over to the kitchenette area on the far side of the lab. She dumped out the lukewarm remains of his coffee, rinsed out the mug, and refilled it with fresh coffee from the pot. Jonathan liked his coffee so strong she could barely tolerate it, and he drank it all day long.

Her back was to the office door, and she pretended to be focused intently on screwing on the lid to his mug.

She swallowed the last of her peppermint. She felt breathless, and her eyes blurred slightly.

She couldn't believe Jonathan was engaged. How was she going to stand working for him every day when he was married, knowing she wasn't even allowed to dream about him?

His fiancée was undoubtedly beautiful—slender, elegant, and stylish. Everything Sarah was not.

"What's wrong?" Jonathan asked from behind her. He'd evidently walked out of his office and taken his normal position at the lab table.

She turned around, her eyes widening. "Nothing. Why?"

Jonathan didn't look anything like a stereotypical research scientist. He was built like a football player, but it must be just good genes because she never saw him working out. He had a strong, handsome face with brown hair and brown eyes, and his clothes and lab coat were perpetually wrinkled.

He gave a half shrug at her question. "You seemed to be having a hard time screwing on the lid."

"Oh. No. I just wasn't paying attention." She smiled at him as brightly as she could as she brought his coffee back over. "Is your uncle doing all right?"

His uncle, Cyrus Damon, had founded a multibillion-dollar conglomerate of hotels and restaurants, and his four nephews were the heirs to his fortune. The other nephews were more in the spotlight than Jonathan. He'd buried himself for years at school at MIT and in the lab here, which he'd opened seven years ago with funding that came primarily from his uncle.

"You heard, huh?" He shook his head as he took a swallow of coffee. "He never changes. He's unhappy with me, as usual."

"I'm sorry to hear that," she murmured, looking back at the DNA sequence blindly. "I didn't know you were engaged. Congratulations." She couldn't help but wonder how he'd found the time to date and get engaged to someone. The one long-term relationship she'd had was with Matt Turner, who'd been hired at the lab at the same time she was. Their relationship had dissolved after a year, in part because they just hadn't had time for each other.

She'd thought Jonathan had nothing in his life but work. Evidently, she'd been wrong.

There was silence beside her, stretching out so long she finally turned. She caught the strangest expression on Jonathan's face.

Half-reluctant and half-guilty.

"What is it?" she prompted. He usually didn't express any emotion at all, his face always relaxed, even when focused deeply on the most minute of genetic details.

"I'm not really engaged."

"What?"

"I lied."

Her belly clenched with a weird combination of relief and excitement. "But he'll have to find out eventually, won't he?"

"I know," he admitted, rubbing his chin in a habitual gesture. She could hear the faint sound of his bristles against his hand. He shaved every day, but he was always bristly again by lunchtime. "It wasn't the smartest of lies. Now he wants me to bring my fictional fiancée to my cousin's wedding."

"I guess you could make up an excuse about why she couldn't come." She tried to sound normal, but she almost felt giddy.

She indulged in daydreams all the time about Jonathan, but she didn't have any realistic hopes about a future with him. He was brilliant, handsome, and would be a billionaire when his uncle died. He commanded attention everywhere he went—so compelling was the force of his intellectual confidence and the depth of his commitment to his goals. It wasn't arrogance or intimidation, and it was completely unconscious on his part. But she'd seen him at conferences and symposiums, and she'd seen the most skeptical of stodgy academics look at him with respect, despite his youth and despite the fact that he wasn't affiliated with a university.

Jonathan Damon could have any woman he wanted. Sarah was smart and was good at her job, but otherwise she was nothing special. She could be content with what she had—a career she'd always dreamed of and working daily with a man as brilliant and amazing as him.

Anything more was a Cinderella dream, and she'd always known that could never happen to her.

"Yeah," Jonathan replied, sitting down on a stool and turning back and forth on it restlessly. "Hopefully he'll accept the excuse. He threatened to pull our funding because I was too focused on research to settle down and get married."

"I heard," she said, surprised he'd told her something so personal. They talked all the time, but it was almost always about work. "It's probably just a passing whim," she added, "brought on by your cousin getting married. You can just make up an excuse for her now and then later claim that she broke the engagement. You don't really think he'll stop funding us, do you?"

He didn't answer immediately, just looked away, which was answer enough.

"Is he really so… so old-fashioned?" She chose her words carefully since she didn't want to offend him. "I mean, to insist that you not stay single."

"Old-fashioned doesn't even begin to describe him. He's an American, like the rest of the family, but he wants to be an eighteenth-century lord of the manor in England." There was a slight bitterness in his brown eyes as he said the words—something she'd never seen there before. He was usually such an even-tempered man.

Since she was feeling jittery, she reached into her drawer for another peppermint, fidgeting with the plastic wrapper after she popped it into her mouth. Jonathan stocked the peppermint balls for her, but neither ever mentioned it. When she first started working for him, she'd tried to thank him for the nice little things he did, but any sort of thanks would make him grumpy for the rest of the day, which for him meant withdrawn and quiet.

So his stocking her peppermint balls went uncommented upon. Not unnoticed though.

"Maybe you could ask a friend to pose as your fiancée," she suggested. "Just for the wedding. That way, you can extend the engagement as long as possible before you say it's called off. By then, maybe he'd feel so sorry for you about the broken engagement that the funding would be safe."

Jonathan arched his eyebrows. "Who would agree to do something so crazy as pretend to be my fiancée?"

"I'd do it," she volunteered without thinking. Mostly, she was trying to make him feel better, and she didn't think through the implications until the words were spoken.

Her cheeks grew hot, and she lowered her eyes to the peppermint wrapper she still held. "I mean, if you decided you wanted to do it."

"You would? Really?"

When she snuck a glance at him, she saw with relief that his expression was speculative rather than disgusted or shocked.

"You'd be willing to do that for me?" he asked after staring at her for a long moment.

"Sure," she said, trying for casual. "Why not? My job is on the line too. It wouldn't be that hard. What would it be? Just a few days?"

"A week," he said, rubbing his chin as if he were already thinking through a to-do list. "My uncle has in mind a prolonged house party."

"Well, that's okay." She made sure she sounded more confident than she felt since the idea of posing as his fiancée for a whole week was absolutely terrifying. How would someone as plain and no-nonsense as her ever pull it off? "If you want to do it, I'm in."

"I'd need to arrive at his place this Friday."

She swallowed hard. She hadn't expected it to be so soon. She was thinking she'd have weeks to prepare or for some kind of natural disaster to occur that would prevent her from going through with it. "No problem. It would just mean putting this project on hold." She nodded toward the microscope they'd been working with before his uncle had called.

He sighed with a very faint twist of his lips. If she hadn't known him so well, she wouldn't have recognized the expression as reluctance. "Yeah. But if we lose our funding, it won't matter. Better to delay now." He hesitated, obviously trying to make the decision.

"I really don't mind. It might be fun. I've never been to England, you know."

"I don't know how fun it will be. You don't know my family. They're a little... high maintenance. Are you sure you'd be comfortable with this? I don't want to put you in an awkward position."

"Why would it be awkward? We're friends, aren't we?"

She wasn't sure where she got the courage to be so daring, to say something so presumptuous. She thought of him as a friend, but they'd never done friend-type things. They'd traveled around Iceland together over the past couple of years, but that was to collect genealogical and genetic information, so it was always under the context of work.

Otherwise, both of them spent all their days and most of their evenings working in this lab.

"Yeah," he agreed, making up his mind at last. "Thanks. I really appreciate this."

She shrugged again, pleased that her casual act was convincing. Maybe she was a better actress than she thought. "Not a problem. I'd hate for you to lose your funding and for me to lose my job. I actually kind of like it, you know."

He smiled at her—a real smile, the one she only saw rarely. For a moment, he was so attractive she almost lost her breath. "Good. Me too."

He took another long gulp of coffee, and they went back to work. Neither mentioned the fake engagement again, and Sarah was quite sure that it had completely slipped out of Jonathan's mind. When he was absorbed in work, he thought about nothing else.

She'd never met anyone who could focus so intently for so long as him.

They worked late since they were making good progress, and it was almost ten in the evening when Sarah realized she was famished and so tired she couldn't see straight. Having a peppermint ball every half hour wasn't cutting it. She hated to call it quits before Jonathan, but sometimes she just had to.

"I'm sorry," she said at last, rolling her chair back over to her desk to set down her tablet. The wheel on her chair had been acting up, and it steered her off course so she almost ran into the corner of a table. "What did you say?" He'd been talking, but she hadn't tracked with any of his words. Her head ached and her stomach churned, and her damned chair wasn't working right.

Jonathan glanced at his watch as if he just realized it was late. "You're exhausted," he said. "Go on home. We'll pick up again tomorrow."

She let out a relieved breath, but still felt a bit guilty. "I can hold out a little longer if you—"

"No, no. It's late. Sorry I kept you so long."

She got up to leave since he'd already gotten distracted again, jotting down notes on his pad of paper as he studied the monitor. But she'd been thinking a lot for the past several hours, and before she left, she had to clear up a few things.

"This wedding. It's going to be really fancy, isn't it?"

He blinked as if he'd just remembered they'd talked about that earlier today. "Yeah."

"I'll need to do some shopping. Is it all right if I have a day off sometime this week to go into Reykjavik?"

"Why do you need to go shopping?"

Her lips parted slightly as she stared at him. "Are you serious? I don't dress up around here. I don't have anything close to appropriate to wear."

"Oh." He wrinkled his forehead as if shopping were something foreign to his experience. "I guess so. Sure, take whatever day you want. Or better yet, we can leave a day early, and you can shop in London. I'll be happy to pay—"

"No," she interrupted, stiffening her shoulders. "I have plenty of money for my clothes. But London would be great. Thanks."

He peered at her like she was an odd specimen under the microscope. "I didn't mean to offend you. I just thought, since you're doing this for me, it would be only fair—"

"I know," she interrupted. "But it would be weird if you bought my clothes. I can buy them myself. You pay me well, and I hardly spend anything here."

It was true. She worked all day almost every day, so she spent almost nothing on recreation or a social life. The lab provided food and housing for its staff since they were in such an isolated part of Iceland. Her generous salary had been accumulating in her bank account for the past three years, and she'd already paid off her student loans.

"I hope you don't mind that I'm not beautiful and glamorous," she said, the words tumbling out before she could stop them. She couldn't help imagining herself among the well-dressed, sophisticated guests at the wedding, and it wasn't a pretty picture.

Sarah wasn't particularly shy, and she was confident about her intellect and the trajectory of her career. She knew she was better looking than she'd been as a child, but she was realistic about herself, and beautiful and glamorous she wasn't.

Normally, it didn't matter. In the life she lived here, it didn't matter if she wasn't attractive. It simply wasn't a relevant factor of her existence since Jonathan was obviously never going to think about her as a woman. But it *would* be relevant at a fancy house party at Damon Manor.

Jonathan stared at her. "What?"

She felt herself flushing again but pressed on. "I mean, I'm sure you would prefer to have a beautiful and glamorous fake fiancée. So I hope you won't mind that I'm not."

"Oh." He blinked as if he'd finally processed what she'd said. "What do I care about that? My uncle wouldn't expect me to get engaged to someone like that. You'll be fine."

"Oh. Good." She went to her desk to get her purse and tried to convince herself she didn't feel disappointed that he'd agreed she wasn't beautiful or glamorous.

It would have been crazy if he'd thought she was.

~

Three hours later, Jonathan realized he'd made a huge mistake.

He'd fixed the bad wheel on Sarah's chair and then had gone to run on the treadmill with his normal reading material—an alternating stack of scientific journals and comic books. Instead of taking mental notes and shaking his head over how half the work his colleagues produced was utter crap, his mind kept drifting over to the upcoming wedding and how it would work for Sarah to pose as his fiancée.

He switched to a comic book, hoping it would better hold his attention.

He'd never really been comfortable around women. Sex was good—since it didn't require much talking and didn't take much time away from work—but relationships had always stumped him. Women either bored him to tears or spent way too much time trying to get him to open up and share his feelings. He was happy to work with women as much as men—he worked better with Sarah than he ever had anyone else—as long as they didn't try to transform the work into something more personal.

He sped up on the treadmill, wiping sweat from his forehead with the back of his hand, his feet pounding on the track as his mind drifted further from his reading.

He'd learned early in life that work was the thing that could bring him fulfillment. His parents were always traveling, so they'd put him in an exclusive boarding school in Switzerland. Whenever he achieved in school, they'd been pleased, so he focused all his effort on academic achievements. They'd died in a plane crash when he was almost eleven, and he'd briefly hoped his uncle could be a father figure for him. His uncle had kept him in the school, however, per his parents' wishes, he had said.

Jonathan had suspected his uncle simply didn't want him.

He spent most of his time in high school studying, and the same was true in college and grad school. When he proposed the purpose and direction of his lab, Cyrus Damon had been impressed and had decided to fund it, but evidently Jonathan hadn't lived up to his uncle's expectations in the rest of his life.

Which wasn't really surprising. He'd never been able to do anything good enough to be a real Damon.

But maybe the fake fiancée plan would be enough to get him back into his uncle's good graces and protect the lab. Without his uncle's money, Jonathan would have to try to find another source of funding, and that would mean giving over control to someone else—who would likely take the research in a direction influenced by money, the market, or politics, which was exactly what Jonathan had been able to avoid thus far.

He knew what he needed to work toward now. Restore his uncle's good opinion. Sustain funding in the lab. Do the work that really mattered.

He and Sarah had always worked well together. If they could treat this house party like a job, like a task to be done, then maybe it wouldn't be so bad.

He was just about to resign the topic to his satisfaction and focus on the adventures of a dark, conflicted superhero when he realized that there was a problem he hadn't even considered before.

He stopped the treadmill, wiped the sweat off his face with a towel, and went down the hall of the staff housing building to Sarah's apartment.

Knocking on the door, he wondered how he could have been so stupid.

It was a minute before she opened the door, and when she did, Jonathan stared at her in astonishment.

Her thick red hair was tumbled messily around her shoulders instead of pulled back in the ponytail she normally wore. And instead of jeans and a sweater, she wore a white tank top and loose cotton pajama pants. She was barefoot, and her blue eyes were groggy and disoriented. She'd clearly just gotten out of bed.

"What's wrong?" she asked, obviously anxious. Her cheeks were flushed, and she crossed her arms in front of her chest. "Is everything all right?"

"Yeah," he said, stunned by how pretty she looked. Pretty and curvy. She always dressed in heavy sweaters and a lab coat, so he'd had no idea she had a body that curved so deliciously. "Sorry. Did I wake you up?"

She glanced at her wrist, although she wasn't wearing a watch. Then she looked behind her shoulder at a clock that showed it was after one in the morning. Instead of complaining about his rudeness, she said, "It's no problem. What's going on?"

"I wasn't thinking before," he explained, pulling himself together so she wouldn't think he was a complete spaz. "I can't let you pose as my fiancée."

"Why not?"

"It wouldn't be fair to Matt. I'm sure he won't like this. I'm not sure why I didn't think of it before."

"Matt?" she asked, pushing up one strap of her top that kept slipping down her shoulder.

"Matt," he repeated, trying not to look at the generous amount of cleavage revealed by the slipping of her tank top. Where the hell had *that* come from? "Your boyfriend? It wouldn't be right for us to do this. I can think of something else."

She stared at him like he'd grown a second head. "I'm not dating Matt anymore."

"What?"

"We broke up almost two years ago. How could you not know that?"

Jonathan froze, trying to rack his brain. Had he heard about the breakup and forgot about it? Surely not. He would have noticed if Sarah had moved from the "Taken" compartment in his mind.

He'd always been comfortable with her since she was smart, accommodating, and had the same priorities he did. She worked for him and was thus off-limits for deep friendship or dating, so he didn't have to worry about dealing with anything personal. For the first few months, she'd tried to thank him all the time and made a big deal about trivial things, which he hadn't liked at all. But since then, she'd always been perfectly safe and comfortable.

Until now, for some reason.

"Did you tell me?" he asked.

She shrugged, glancing down almost shyly, which struck him as uncharacteristic. And kind of pretty. "I don't know. Maybe not. But I figured you'd know. *Everyone* knew."

It was true that no one had any privacy in the lab. In such a closed community, keeping a secret was almost impossible, but he usually just ignored the gossip since it wasn't of any interest to him.

"So you don't have a boyfriend?"

"No," she said, adjusting the wayward strap again and in the process hiding some of the cleavage. "It's totally fine. It's no big deal. Really."

"Okay. Good." He stood for a moment, still feeling rather disoriented, like his precariously balanced world was starting to wobble.

Unfortunately, in the process of staring, he noticed that he could see the outline of her nipples beneath the thin fabric of her top.

He really didn't need to see that.

Her breasts were gorgeous, full and rounded, their shape easily visible beneath the clingy fabric. His body obviously liked the look of them, which was totally wrong.

He'd tried to date when he first set up the lab here in Iceland, but there weren't many women around that matched his intellect and interests, and soon it was more trouble than it was worth. So he'd lived like a monk for the past three years. It wasn't an ideal situation, but his urges were simply physical. There were ways to take care of those urges that didn't interfere with work.

But his body knew it was being deprived and was clearly taking revenge by reacting quite wrongly to Sarah now.

"Is everything all right?" she asked, peering at him in concern.

"Yeah. Sorry. That is, sorry I woke you up."

"So we're still on for the trip?"

"Yeah. If you're not with Matt anymore, then I guess it's fine."

"Great." Her eyes scanned over him, as if she'd just noticed his condition. "Why are you all sweaty?"

"I was on the treadmill," he explained, gesturing with the comic book he still held, as if that would explain why his T-shirt was sticking wetly to his chest.

She peered at the comic book, her lips turning up in a smile. "I didn't know you ran on the treadmill. Is that what you always read?"

He glanced down at it almost sheepishly. He'd managed for three years to keep his habits private, even from the person he worked most closely with. He hated to be slotted into the geek stereotype, although in some ways he supposed he fit. He raised his eyebrows almost haughtily. "Is there something wrong with that?"

"Of course not." Her lips quivered.

"Since, if I'm not mistaken, you have the entire seven seasons of a television series about a girl who kills vampires prominently displayed back there, I don't think you have any grounds to be snide about my reading material." He gestured with his head toward the shelf against the far wall, pleased he had something to counter with.

She flushed again and glanced back at them guiltily, although her lips were still trembling with humor. "I wouldn't dream of being snide. I'll let you get back to the treadmill. I'm going back to sleep now."

"Good. Great. Thanks."

He must sound like an absolute idiot, he realized when she shut the door. For the first time since he'd known her, the thought of Sarah made him a little uncomfortable.

And he thought of pretending to be engaged to her for a whole ten days with his family made him *very* uncomfortable.

CHAPTER TWO

Sarah woke up in a strange room.

She took a minute to orient herself to the crisp bedding and high-end furnishings until she remembered she was in the bedroom of the luxury London hotel she and Jonathan had checked into last night.

Sarah's parents were squarely middle class, and she'd been raised staying only at midlevel chain hotels. This room was much nicer than anything she was accustomed to.

She sat up in bed, feeling fuzzy and vaguely nervous.

She and Jonathan had flown into London the evening before, arriving so late they hadn't done anything but go to bed. He'd reserved a two-bedroom suite, explaining that he didn't want anyone to wonder why an engaged couple was staying in separate rooms. Since he was a Damon, people might be paying attention.

Sarah would have preferred an entirely separate room—since it would be very easy for her to start thinking in dangerous directions here—but she didn't want to risk exposing their charade, so she hadn't complained.

She had a headache, so instead of jumping right in the shower as she'd planned, she put on a soft hoodie over her tank top, pulled her messy hair into a quick ponytail, and went out to the main room of the suite to get a cup of coffee.

Maybe Jonathan wouldn't be up yet.

He was up, sitting near the window, drinking coffee out of his travel mug, and working on his laptop. He'd thrown on some clothes but obviously hadn't showered or shaved.

"Morning," she said brightly, trying to sound casual despite the weird fluttery nerves she felt over seeing him so domestically first thing in the morning.

"Hey. You're up early."

"Not as early as you. Did you sleep at all?"

He shrugged, still focusing on his laptop. "A couple of hours."

Sarah added a lot of cream to her coffee since he'd made it as strong as usual. "What are you working on?" He didn't usually spend much time on the computer, so she was curious.

"E-mail. Nothing else to do outside the lab."

Sarah had learned early on not to send Jonathan e-mail since he would rarely answer it. She sipped her coffee, watching as he rubbed his chin and read something on his screen. He hated e-mail, just like he hated shaving and eating lunch—tedious duties that distracted him from the work he really cared about.

He glanced over, noticing her watching him. "Do you think you'll be done with shopping by four this afternoon? My uncle wants us there by dinner. If not, I'll just tell him no."

Sarah almost snorted. "Definitely. I've never shopped more than an hour in my life. If I make it to noon, it will be a remarkable feat." As she talked, she walked over to him and checked his mug. It was almost empty, so she brought it over to the kitchenette to refill it.

He looked away from his screen again with a smile that made her flush with pleasure since he obviously appreciated that she was low maintenance about shopping.

He accepted the coffee she handed him automatically, barely registering that his mug had been filled. He appeared to be in a friendly mood, so she sat down on the sofa near his chair to drink her coffee. Her headache was already starting to go away.

Jonathan was way too attractive this morning, his T-shirt stretched across his broad shoulders and strong arms, and the stubble and messy hair making him look rumpled and masculine.

She'd never realized he worked out, but she now realized that was foolish. He wouldn't be in such good shape otherwise. He must do it right before bed. When he'd knocked on her door in the middle of the night earlier this week, he'd been hot and sweaty and sexy.

It was so strange seeing him out of a lab coat—like he wasn't fully dressed even though he was completely covered.

Another flutter of nerves made her ask, "Do you think we'll have separate rooms at your uncle's?"

He looked up again, vaguely surprised. "Yeah. For sure. He never puts unmarried persons in the same room."

"Okay. I should have guessed since you'd said he was so old-fashioned." She hid her relief. Having her own room would be much better. The less she saw of Jonathan like this, the better.

Imagining what he'd be like in bed was really not good for her state of mind.

She noticed a newspaper lying on a side table, so she opened it up to read. A few minutes later, she glanced over at Jonathan and noticed he was watching her.

She was glad she'd put on the hoodie so she was completely covered. She was in her pajamas but wasn't showing any more skin than in her work clothes.

She cringed as she thought back to the other night, when she had been too startled by the knock to think about covering up.

Some women went around in tank tops all the time, but she'd never been skinny enough for that. She wasn't fat—by no definition could she be considered fat—but she also wasn't skinny, and she didn't like to show off her body.

She started to grow uncomfortable, so she got up to refill her coffee and then told Jonathan she was going to get dressed.

He mumbled out an inarticulate response. He was focused on work again, so she wasn't even sure he noticed she left the room.

~

Sarah stared at herself in the mirror with a heavy feeling in her gut.

She really didn't like what she saw.

"I guess it's all right," she said, turning slightly to see her ass in the three-paneled mirror.

The saleswoman, whose name was Karen, shook her head. "It's not good. The black washes you out, and the A-line skirt makes you look hippy."

"I *am* hippy," Sarah responded mournfully.

She had no idea where the best place in London was to shop, so she'd gone to a well-known department store. The clothes were more expensive than she'd expected, there were way too many departments, and she wasn't even sure what she'd need. She'd wandered around aimlessly for nearly an hour, feeling more and more anxious about how she would ever get decent clothes for this wedding. She was going to humiliate herself and Jonathan.

Karen had found her close to tears over a rack of cocktail dresses and offered to help. Sarah had explained her predicament and was vastly relieved when Karen told her she was in the right place since she'd definitely need a couple of cocktail dresses for dinners or drinks.

"Can I pick out something for you?" Karen asked. "Would you mind?"

"Sure," Sarah said. "If you think something would be better than this. But I'll need black, won't I? I don't want to stand out."

"Hold on. I'll be right back."

Sarah returned to the dressing cubicle, took off the unflattering dress, and waited until Karen flopped another dress over the door.

"Navy blue is just as good as black," Karen explained, sounding like she was really getting excited about the challenge of finding Sarah something to wear.

Sarah was glad one of them was having fun.

"The blue will bring out your eyes," Karen added. "Try it on."

"It's too short," Sarah squeaked, holding up the simple sheath dress. "And my arms aren't thin enough to pull off the sleeveless look."

"Try it on," Karen said. "How do you know what will look good on you if you haven't tried?"

Sarah grumbled to herself as she pulled on the dress, and she cringed as she contorted to zip it up in the back. It was far more fitted than anything she ever wore. Not to mention short. And sleeveless. If she was a size four, she would have liked this dress.

She wasn't a size four.

When she looked in the mirror, it wasn't as bad as she expected though.

"Let me see," Karen demanded.

Sarah self-consciously came out to the large mirror in the dressing area, hoping no other shoppers were around to see her.

"It's great," Karen said, clapping her hands. "You just need some heels. What size do you wear?"

Sarah told her and peered in the mirror dubiously. The soft fabric skimmed her body, emphasizing the curves of her breasts and waist in a flattering way. Her arms weren't as bad as she'd thought—she actually liked the graceful curve of her shoulders and neck. And when Karen arrived with a pair of stylish heels, Sarah's legs actually looked pretty good.

"See," Karen said, grinning. "I told you."

Sarah almost laughed, feeling a slowly rising giddiness at the thought of almost looking pretty. "My skin is too white though. Don't you think? My legs look strange. Do you think I should wear tights or... do women still wear pantyhose?"

Karen frowned, thinking. "Some do, but... Oh, I know. Hold on."

Sarah waited, admiring herself from every angle and pleased that even her ass didn't look too huge, although the curve of it was definitely visible.

Karen came back with a smile that was almost naughty. "Here—try these."

Sarah gaped at the package the other woman handed her. They were expensive, delicate, lace-topped stockings.

"You've got to be kidding me," she said at last.

"I'm not kidding. They're very sexy."

"Do people still wear these?"

"They're back in style. They'd look great on you."

"Do I need a garter belt or whatever it's called to hold them up?"

"No, no. You'd be able to see the outline of it through that dress. These stay up on their own."

"But... I'll feel silly."

"You're going to a Damon house party, aren't you? I'm telling you, these won't be out of place, and they'll be better than trying to wear tights all the time. I'd go with these or just bare legged."

Sarah wasn't about to go bare legged. Her skin was just too white. Girls at school used to tease her about wearing white hose all the time when it had simply been her bare legs.

So she grabbed the package with a frown. Maybe she'd like them more than she thought.

~

It was almost three in the afternoon when Sarah finally got back to the hotel. She'd needed a bellboy to help her with all her purchases. She'd spent a small fortune at the department store, but she was very pleased with the results.

Karen had talked her into trying things on she never would have done on her own, like the brown pencil skirt she wore now with a moss-green cashmere twin set, two-tone heels, and a string of pearls.

Cyrus Damon expected people to make an effort, Karen had explained. Evidently, everyone knew that. He wouldn't want someone arriving at his estate in jeans, even if they'd been traveling all day.

Jonathan wore tan trousers and a dress shirt that was only slightly wrinkled, so he'd obviously made an effort too. He was still working on his laptop, and he just glanced over with a "hello" when she arrived.

"Looks like you found a lot," he said, taking a gulp of his coffee. His mug was obviously almost empty, since he had to turn it almost upside down to get the last sip out.

29

Sarah tipped the bellboy and then fussed around with her bags. She'd had to buy new luggage too since she'd never be able to fit all this in the bag she'd brought with her from Iceland.

She waited for Jonathan to notice how nice she looked.

A couple of minutes later, she realized she was waiting in vain. He was obviously caught up in whatever he was working on.

So she started lugging bags to her room with a sigh.

She was about to turn around to get another load of bags, but Jonathan had gotten up and was hauling the rest of them for her. At least he wasn't so oblivious he'd forgotten to be nice.

He dropped the bags on the floor of her room as he stared at her.

He'd obviously just realized her appearance had changed.

She glanced down at herself self-consciously. Her pretty clothes were all still in place. She got a happy shiver when she saw them.

"What did you do?" he asked at last.

"What did I *do?*" she repeated, a wave of disappointment washing over her. His face reflected no pleasure or admiration at all. Just surprise. "What do you think I did? I got new clothes. And a haircut."

She'd gone up to the salon on the top floor of the department store. They'd cut off several inches of her hair and given it some long layers. Since it was lighter than normal, it waved rather than bushed out. The stylist had suggested some lowlights to deepen the red color, and she'd agreed. She'd also agreed to an eyebrow wax, a manicure and a pedicure. She felt absolutely gorgeous when she'd left the department store at last, and she'd never felt that way before.

It would have been nice if Jonathan noticed.

"Oh," he said, blinking and eyeing her from top to bottom like she was a bizarre creature in a museum. "You look…"

She waited for him to finish. "Gorgeous" would make her happy. "Pretty" would be satisfying. "Nice," would be all right and probably more characteristic of him.

"Different."

Sarah froze for a moment, registering what he'd said. Then she turned away, hiding her hurt feelings.

It didn't matter what he thought. He didn't have to like how she looked. She'd always known that Jonathan Damon would never fall for her.

She just didn't want to embarrass herself or him at the fancy house party.

Maybe someone else would think she was pretty.

~

Sarah looked like a gorgeous stranger, and Jonathan didn't like it at all.

She looked elegant, like she might belong in his uncle's social circle—something Jonathan had never felt himself. That idea made him uncomfortable.

She also looked incredibly lush and sexy, despite the demure, ladylike outfit. The skirt emphasized her ass in a way he'd never noticed before, and the soft cashmere clung to her breasts. She made him think about sex, and that was even more uncomfortable.

Sarah was incredibly important to his work—he couldn't at the moment imagine doing his job without her—so he couldn't allow himself to ever think about her in any other way.

Hopefully, she wouldn't look so irresistible for the entire coming week.

His uncle had sent a car and driver to pick them up, and he'd brought a scientific journal to pass the time on the drive to the estate. That normally would have been enough to distract him from any uncomfortable thoughts, but he kept noticing Sarah shifting beside him on the seat. He kept smelling a light, fresh fragrance that was obviously her.

She was never one to make small talk, only speaking if she had something to say. He'd always liked that about her, but now the silence was strangely oppressive.

Something seemed to be the matter with her, but he had no idea what it was.

Finally, he put down the journal with a sigh, wishing he'd thought to bring his coffee with him.

He glanced over at Sarah. Her shoulders were stiff and her face pointed away from him. "Is this going to be okay?" he asked, wondering why he'd been so idiotic as to think this ridiculous scheme would ever work.

She looked at him in surprise. "Of course. Why wouldn't it be?"

He lowered his brows. "Are you all right?" Her eyes looked bluer than they ever had before, maybe because of the sunlight rather than the artificial light of the lab. But her eyes also looked like she was close to tears.

He didn't like that at all. She'd always been happy and agreeable. He didn't like that she was upset. He needed to fix it.

"What's wrong?" he asked, when she didn't respond.

She gave a huff, almost poignant amusement. "Nothing."

He frowned. She was obviously lying. "Tell me."

She cleared her throat and slid her eyes away from him. "It's nothing really," she admitted, almost self-consciously. "I just spent a lot of time and effort today, trying to look nice."

"You do look nice," he said in surprise. "Who said you didn't?" He felt a sudden flash of defensive resentment at the thought of someone putting her down. He had no idea where the feeling came from, but Sarah was *his*—his assistant, his help, and companion—and he was irrationally angry at the thought of anyone not appreciating her appropriately.

After a long moment, to his absolute astonishment, Sarah started to laugh. Freely. Uninhibitedly. Her amusement was so infectious and so pretty he couldn't look away, even though he had no idea what was causing it.

"What's so funny?" he asked at last.

"Nothing," she gasped, wiping away a couple of stray tears. "Sorry. It's really nothing."

She was acting confusing, something she'd never been before. He wasn't quite sure why this was happening.

He was relieved when she changed the subject.

"What are your cousins like?"

"They're okay. I'm not very close to them."

"You grew up with them?"

He gave a half shrug. "Not really. My parents died in the same plane crash as Andrew and Harrison's parents, so my uncle became the guardian of all of us at the same time. But I was at school most of the time, and they had each other."

"Were they nice to you?"

"They made an effort, but we didn't have a lot of in common. I don't mind them. We're just not close."

"Did you fight a lot?"

He shrugged again. "Not that much. One year at Christmas, we went skiing, and they were so mad because I could ski better than them. They were used to being better at sports than me."

"You're a good skier?" She looked surprised.

He wondered if she thought he wasn't good at anything active. She'd been surprised he was running on the treadmill earlier that week. He didn't like that idea either. Surely she realized he was a man capable of physical activity outside a research lab. "I went to school in Switzerland. We skied a lot."

"What about Benjamin? That's your other cousin, right?"

"Yeah. He lived in the States with his mother, so I never spent much time with him."

"Is he coming to the wedding?"

"I don't know. He was asked, but I doubt he'll come. He hasn't said a word to my uncle in years."

"That's too bad. So you didn't get closer to your cousins after you grew up?"

"We have different lives. It's not like they were my brothers."

The truth was, there had been a time when he would have liked to be close to them, but nothing he'd ever done had impressed them. He figured they'd always just written him off as a science nerd.

For some reason, the thought made him remember something. Reluctantly, he reached into his pocket and pulled out a little velvet pouch.

"Before I forget, you better wear this, since we're supposed to be engaged." He dumped a ring out onto his palm and handed it to her.

He'd spent a ludicrous amount of time that morning picking out an engagement ring. He'd gone to a smallish jewelry store, which he thought might expedite the process. He'd assumed it would be a simple decision, but the salesperson kept asking him questions about Sarah, trying to get a ring that fit her personality.

So the ring-shopping trip had taken much longer than he'd expected, and he'd had to think about Sarah and her personality much more deeply than he was normally inclined to do.

So he was strangely hesitant about offering her the final choice.

It had a delicately filigreed band of white and yellow gold with one square-shaped diamond.

Sarah stared down at the ring with wide eyes.

"Is it okay?" he asked at last.

"It's gorgeous. You didn't have to—"

"You had to have a ring."

"Oh. Right. But it looks too expensive."

He shrugged. It had been very expensive, but he'd never cared much about money one way or the other except when it interfered with his work.

"It's beautiful."

He frowned, feeling like an idiot still holding out his hand with the untaken ring. At least she seemed to like it.

When she still made no move to take it, he demanded, "Would you just take the stupid thing?"

"Oh. Yeah. Sorry." She was flushed, her hair hanging down over her face. "Thank you."

Feeling awkward and ridiculous, he watched her slide the ring onto her ring finger. They both stared down at how it looked.

"It's beautiful," she murmured again.

He glanced away, feeling more uncomfortable than ever. He wished she wouldn't make a big deal about it.

Then Sarah said, "We should probably decide on a backstory in case people ask us how we got together and how we got engaged and everything. If we keep it simple, it shouldn't be too hard."

Jonathan was relieved to have a task to work on, and the rest of the trip wasn't so unsettling.

~

Gordon, Cyrus Damon's long-standing butler, answered the door, smiling at Jonathan with a placid face and kind blue eyes.

Jonathan had always liked Gordon. In fact, he was the only member of the household Jonathan was really looking forward to seeing. But he felt weirdly guilty as he introduced him to Sarah, calling her his fiancée.

It seemed wrong to lie to a man like Gordon.

Gordon greeted Sarah with kind professionalism, said Mr. Damon was on a conference call but would be out to greet them as soon as possible, and then he showed them up to a room on the second floor of the west wing of the mansion.

It was a large, ornate room with a huge old-fashioned bed and lush fabrics. Gordon gestured both of them in, however, and then the footman trailing them brought their luggage—*both* of their luggage—into the one room.

"Will this be all right?" Gordon asked, obviously reading something in Jonathan's stunned face.

"I didn't think he would want us to share a room."

Gordon's mouth twitched just slightly with what looked like amusement. "Of course, his preference would be to offer separate rooms. But we're tight on space because of the number of guests expected, and since you are engaged to Dr. Stratford, he decided this would be appropriate."

Jonathan shot a glance to Sarah.

She was slightly flushed, but she smiled at Gordon. "This is lovely. Thanks so much."

Gordon looked faintly relieved and told them that dinner was at seven.

That was obviously a reminder that they shouldn't be late.

When they were alone, Jonathan looked at Sarah. "I'm sorry about this. I can't believe he's okay with putting us in the same room. I can sleep on the floor." He glanced around and noticed a chaise near the window. "Or on that."

"Don't be silly," Sarah said, far more casually than she felt. "We're both adults and the bed is big. It won't be any trouble to share it."

Jonathan agreed, since there was no reason not to. But he couldn't help but think things were becoming far more intimate than he'd expected, far more intimate than was appropriate for two people who worked together the way they did.

Sarah leaned down to get something out of a bag. "You'll put something else on for dinner, won't you? I mean, they dress up for dinner more than we're dressed up now?"

"Yeah. Usually."

"We should say hello to your uncle first though, right? Before we start to get dressed. Will you take a shower?"

Her quick-fire questions sounded a little nervous, and he wondered if sharing a room had upset her more than she'd let on. Jonathan watched as she rooted around for something, instinctively taking note of the lush curve of her ass. Then he noticed, as her skirt hiked up some, the lace top of one of her stockings.

His body reacted to the sultry look of the old-fashioned stockings on lovely legs he'd never even noticed before.

She always just been Sarah—smart, competent, thoughtful, eminently comfortable. Exactly the kind of person he wanted to work with. Exactly the kind of woman he wanted to spend his days with. How she'd turned into this curvy, sexy creature, he had no idea.

But his body was responding very inappropriately, and they were going to have to share a bed.

He was definitely taking a shower before dinner. Maybe right now.

And he'd probably be taking another one before bed.

CHAPTER THREE

Sarah woke up early since she'd gone to bed early the night before. After dinner, Jonathan had said he was going to work out in the gym in the basement. Thinking it would be less awkward to go to bed when he wasn't around, Sarah had taken a quick shower and gotten in bed.

He must have done something other than work out since he hadn't come to bed until almost three in the morning. Sarah had half awoken when he'd climbed under the covers beside her but had been too groggy to feel nervous about it.

He was still asleep now, having just gotten to bed a couple of hours ago. She snuck a look over at him.

He slept on his side, facing her, so she could see his relaxed face, mussed hair, and bare chest. The sheet was sliding down toward his waist, so she could see *a lot* of his chest.

She jumped out of bed at the intense way the sight of his sleeping beside her affected her.

Despite how deeply she knew it was wrong—knew it was impossible—she wanted to wake up next to him every day. She couldn't seem to help it.

She showered quickly, and even with the extra time it spent to manage her new hairstyle, she was ready in just a half hour. Since Jonathan still slept, she grabbed her phone and went downstairs.

The house was quiet. Breakfast wouldn't be served for another thirty minutes. She wanted to walk around the gardens, but she stood at the front door hesitantly, afraid if she opened it an alarm would start blaring.

"I turn off security at five in the mornings," a quiet voice came from behind her.

She turned to see Gordon. He held a silver teapot and smiled at her pleasantly.

She smiled back, relieved. "Oh, good. Thank you. I'm just going to walk around the gardens, if that's all right."

"Of course, Dr. Stratford. You're more than welcome. If you'd like breakfast early—"

"Oh, no. Thank you. And please, you can call me Sarah."

His smile seemed to deepen, although it was only reflected in his eyes. "Thank you, ma'am. But I really can't."

She must not have offended him with her gaff, so she didn't feel too embarrassed. She walked outside, found the formal gardens around the back and strolled them, gawking at the pristine beds, immaculately trimmed hedges, elegant statuary, and intricate Rococo fountain while she called her parents.

They didn't go to bed until around midnight, so it was early enough to call safely, even with the time difference.

They always put her on speaker phone so they could both hear what she had to say. She told her mother about some of the new clothes she'd bought and her father about some of the progress they'd made on their research. She told them she was in England on a work trip but, since she didn't

41

want them to worry, she didn't tell them exactly what she was doing. They told her that her sister and her husband were putting in a pool in their backyard and about how her three nephews and one niece were doing in school.

She felt better after she talked to them—as she always did. Like, no matter how foreign her location or how insecure she was about her current situation, she was grounded by people who loved her no matter what.

When she hung up, she realized it was time for breakfast and a several-minute walk back to the mansion.

She was breathless when she entered the house, afraid she'd been unforgivably rude by arriving late.

Breakfast, however, was evidently different from dinner. People must arrive whenever they wanted. Marietta, the soon-to-be bride, was just coming down the steps as Sarah entered.

Marietta grinned at her. "Good morning! You're out and about early."

"Just taking a walk."

Sarah had been vastly relieved when she'd met Marietta the day before. The other woman was very pretty but not aloof, sophisticated, and ultrastylish as Sarah had feared. She had blond hair, gray eyes, and a sunny smile. She was about Sarah's height and a couple of sizes smaller, but she wasn't built like a model, and she was wearing simple gray trousers and a cute eyelet shirt, which was exactly in line with Sarah's tan pants and green ruched top .

Marietta had a slight, lilting French accent, but she still seemed not very different than the regular people Sarah had grown up with.

"I'm starving," Marietta said companionably. "They always serve the best breakfasts here."

As Sarah responded, they entered the breakfast room and saw that both Jonathan and Harrison, Marietta's fiancé, were already at the table.

Jonathan was reading a journal, and Harrison—a little taller and leaner than Jonathan but just as handsome—appeared to be going through e-mail on his tablet.

Jonathan barely glanced up when she came in.

She wasn't surprised—she knew how much he focused on whatever took his attention, so much that the rest of the world faded away. She went to fill up a plate and pour herself a cup of coffee and brought it over to sit beside him.

"You two are very social, I see," Marietta teased, serving a pile of mixed fruit on her plate. "Practically chatting each other's ears off."

Harrison, who had struck Sarah the night before as very serious and professional, smiled at his fiancée with a soft expression and leaned over to kiss her when she sat down beside him.

Sarah had automatically checked Jonathan's mug and, noticing it was close to empty, went to refill it. But she got a little worried when she came back to sit down.

Jonathan accepted the coffee but still hadn't acknowledged her existence.

They were supposed to be engaged. In love. No one was likely to believe their story if he didn't make a little effort.

Harrison had put his tablet away after a pointed glance from Marietta. Sarah wasn't sure if it was because he wasn't supposed to work during breakfast or if he wasn't supposed to work when there were other people at the table. Either way, he and Marietta chatted with her in a friendly way, asking interested questions about when she'd started working at the lab and where she'd gone to school.

Sarah was able to answer all the questions honestly, which made her feel better—like she wasn't a complete bitch for lying to these nice people.

"Was it hard?" Marietta asked. "Moving all the way to Iceland, I mean?"

"Oh no. We're working most of the time anyway, and Iceland is an ideal location for gene research."

"Why is that?" Harrison asked. His eyes were beautiful—a soft chocolate brown—and he wasn't as intimidating as she'd thought at first.

"Because it's such an restricted gene pool, since the population has been so cut off for so long from the rest of the world. And they're crazy about genealogy. They've got records going back for generations. To do the research we're doing on MS, we couldn't find a better place. It took a while to get used to the winters and summers with the really short days and really long days. But that was the only hard thing for me."

She glanced over toward Jonathan, hoping he would join the conversation and act like he noticed she was in the room. He didn't though, and Sarah didn't miss the amused glances Marietta sent him occasionally, as if she were silently laughing over his behavior.

When she caught Sarah's eye during one of those glances, Marietta explained, "It must be a family trait. For Harry, it's e-mail."

Harrison rolled his eyes, and Sarah just laughed, trying to feign affection when she really wanted to strangle Jonathan for his stupidity.

This was *his* family, *his* scheme. Why wouldn't he rouse himself enough to at least pretend he knew she existed?

She leaned over toward him, much farther into his personal space than she ever went on purpose. Pretending to peer at the page he was reading, she asked, "Good article, dear?"

"Not bad," he murmured absently. "A team in California finished an eight-year project on the—" He broke off as he suddenly realized what she'd called him and how close she was to him. He straightened up.

She tried to give him a discreet, significant look—since they'd never convince anyone they were engaged if he jerked away from her like that—but it must have gone over his head.

"Anyway," he concluded after taking a slug of coffee as if he'd filled in the rest of the information about the article, "the conclusions are promising."

Sarah took the journal from him, pretending to study the article he'd been reading. Then she didn't give it back, tucking it under her thigh on the chair.

He appeared on the verge of objecting, but she silenced him with another look.

When she looked back at Marietta and Harrison, they both seemed amused by this bit of byplay. Maybe they'd assume it was just normal snipping between lovers and not one idiot completely clueless about how to pretend to be engaged.

She wondered what Jonathan would be like when he was really in love. Would he transform into an attentive, adoring boyfriend?

Probably not.

It wasn't like he was selfish or heartless. He noticed a lot when he seemed wrapped up in other things. He'd fixed the wheel on her lab chair earlier that week and hadn't said a word about it. He just wasn't expressive or romantic.

Still, their charade would be more convincing if he'd act like he was in love with her.

There was some noise at the front door, and Marietta jumped up. "Andrew and Laurel must be here at last!"

Sarah had learned last night that Harrison's brother and his girlfriend had planned to arrive the day before, but foul weather had delayed their trip. It was quite clear that both Marietta and Harrison were very pleased about their arrival. Marietta was practically clapping, and the only thing holding Harrison back was courtesy. "My brother," he explained to Sarah, in case she couldn't figure it out. "Would you excuse us for a few minutes?"

"Of course," she said with a smile. "I'm looking forward to meeting them."

Jonathan glanced up but didn't stand.

As Harrison and Marietta left the breakfast room, Sarah poked Jonathan in the arm. Hard.

"What?" he demanded, looking surprised and vaguely annoyed.

"You should go greet your cousin," she said, trying not to sound as annoyed as she felt.

"Okay," he said, frowning as he heaved himself out of his chair. "What are you all riled up about?"

She *was* riled up, so much so that she wasn't able to suppress it like she normally would. She glared at him as they walked toward the door and said under her breath, "We're supposed to be engaged. No one is going to believe it if you keep acting like I don't exist."

"What?" he asked, blinking once the way he did when he was sorting something out in his mind. His dark brown eyes were focused on her now, and she was so close she could see very faint stubble on his chin even though she knew he'd shaved just an hour ago.

"You're acting like I just work with you," she whispered sharply. "You're supposed to be in love with me. I know it's hard, but can you at least try to pretend you're crazy about me?"

He stared at her for a moment, evidently startled at her defiance. He had reason to be since she'd never talked to him that way before. Not once.

They were standing in the entry hall while the new arrivals were being greeted—the man who must be Andrew was hugging Marietta so enthusiastically he'd picked her up. It

47

really wasn't the time for a fight. Sarah should have brought it up later, and she shouldn't have been so vehement. He was still her boss.

And she really didn't want to lose her dream job.

Jonathan's eyes were strange—focused, alive in a way she only saw when he was caught up in research. He didn't respond though. He just reached over, took her face in one of his big hands, and leaned into a kiss.

Sarah was so shocked she couldn't respond immediately. Then she felt a wave of pleasure wash over her as his mouth moved against hers.

She wrapped one arm around his neck instinctively and melted against him.

When he pulled away, she was dazed and breathless and in danger of oozing into a boneless heap on the floor.

"Is that better?" he demanded.

That slapped her back into focus. "That's fine," she said, turning away from him, flustered. She saw that the others had seen them kissing, which was probably good for their scheme but made her flush hotly just the same.

Andrew looked a lot like Harrison but had green eyes instead of brown and was quicker to laugh, quicker to grin. Sarah liked him immediately when he greeted Jonathan enthusiastically with a handshake that turned into a half hug and told her good-naturedly that his cousin didn't deserve someone so smart and beautiful.

It wasn't true, but it was really nice that he'd said it.

But when she shook hands with Laurel, whom he introduced to her in a way that somehow conveyed her preciousness, Sarah was immediately intimidated.

Laurel was as tall and slender as a model, and she was stunningly beautiful, with dark hair, dark eyes, and sculpted cheekbones that looked faintly Native American.

She smiled as they were introduced, but she seemed a lot more aloof than Marietta.

She made Sarah feel, even in her pretty new clothes, like a frumpy plebian.

Laurel and Marietta were obviously close, which made Sarah feel even more like an outsider. She was used to feeling that way—she had all the time at school—but she'd been feeling more comfortable with herself lately, even that morning, so the realization hit her like a blow.

She withdrew, standing beside Jonathan, who looked like he'd rather be elsewhere as well. She was grateful when he put an arm around her waist, even though she knew it was just part of their pretense.

They chatted for a while in the entry hall about the storm, about the trip, about details of the wedding. Laurel was going to be the maid of honor and evidently took her role seriously. She pulled out a file folder with all her duties organized with printouts and to-do lists.

Finally, Gordon suggested that Andrew and Laurel might want to get settled, so the group disbanded.

Jonathan went back into the breakfast room to get his coffee and journal, Sarah assumed. She was going to follow him when Marietta stopped her.

"Laurel and I are going shopping this afternoon for wedding things. Please say you'll come with us."

If Marietta had been just being polite, Sarah wouldn't have accepted, but the other woman's expression was open and sincere.

As if she really did want Sarah to come along.

"Thank you," she said. "I'd love to." She didn't really want to spend another day shopping, but hanging out with the women might be easier than trying to muddle through the pretense with Jonathan. "I need to check with Jonathan, to make sure he didn't have anything planned, but otherwise it would be great."

Jonathan, when asked, said it was fine, so Sarah went shopping two days in a row for the first time in her life.

~

Jonathan wasn't having a very good day.

He was a little annoyed that Sarah had deserted him. He'd been hoping they could do something away from the estate. She hadn't been to England before, so they could have done some sightseeing, which would give him an excuse to not to spend awkward time with his family.

Instead, he had no choice but to accept when his uncle suggested they tour the estate since it had been so long since he'd been there and he'd missed all the latest improvements.

Cyrus Damon was obviously making an effort to be civil, but Jonathan could have done without several hours with his uncle.

It was bad enough that his uncle had always treated his scientific ambitions as second class just because Jonathan hadn't wanted to be involved in the family business. But now he'd forced him to concoct this ludicrous scheme and potentially damage the good working relationship he had with Sarah in order to keep his uncle happy and his lab funded.

If his uncle had cared about him at all, Jonathan would have no complaints about putting up with any number of annoyances and eccentricities. But for Cyrus Damon, it was all about family obligation.

Nothing Jonathan had ever done had been good enough for him.

He made it through the tour of the estate without offending his uncle, and then he was able to escape to the media room for the rest of the afternoon to play Sea and Sky, which used to be his favorite video game. The estate, of course, had all the up-to-date game technology one could hope for, but he dug up the dated game system so he could play his favorite game. He'd stayed up late playing it the night before, instead of going to bed with Sarah, and he'd found it a good distraction.

The women were having dinner in London, so it was just the men that evening. Harrison and Andrew were obviously trying to be friendly, so Jonathan made an effort to respond. They weren't bad. They were just different, and his work wouldn't really impress them. He didn't think he'd ever be really close to them.

By evening, he was irrationally annoyed with Sarah. He was used to having her around all the time. She filled his coffee, reminded him of things he might forget, and otherwise smoothed over rough corners. He could have used her help in dealing with his family, but instead she was off gallivanting on another shopping trip.

How much shopping did a woman need to do? She'd already bought out half of London the day before.

It was late when she got back, and Jonathan was reading in bed. She looked tired and said she was going to take a shower.

Jonathan just nodded and kept reading, hoping that concentrating on the words on the page would help distract him from the thought of Sarah and her lush body getting into the bed with him.

His hopes were not realized. When she came out a few minutes later, she wore a simple pajama set—cream-colored top with lace straps and cotton shorts—but it emphasized the curves of her breasts and hips. She must have just brushed her hair since it hung down in shiny waves around her shoulders.

She looked fresh, pretty, almost innocent—and so sexy his body tightened.

He tried even harder to focus on the tedious findings of a research project he cared nothing about as she walked over and got under the covers beside him.

She smelled like vanilla with an undertone of something fresh like lime. He'd seen the scented lotion on the sink in the bathroom, and the fragrance did something dangerous to his body.

He didn't know what was wrong with him. He'd spent all day, every day with Sarah for the past three years.

He worked with her. He didn't respond to her like *this*.

"How was your day?" she asked, turning out the light on her bedside table. Only his light was still on now, casting strange shadows on the rest of the room.

"Fine." He could feel her moving beside him, and he tried desperately not to think about how her soft body would feel against his.

"Is everything all right?"

It was a familiar question. She asked it of him a lot, usually in response to something going wrong in the lab. Very often, she would have a solution.

She could offer him a solution to his current predicament, but it wasn't one he would ever accept.

He couldn't have sex with her, no matter how much he temporarily wanted to. Their work was too important, and he didn't want to think about trying to do that work without her, which was what would happen if they indulged in an affair.

"Jonathan?" she prompted. She was looking at him— he could feel it—and he realized he hadn't answered her question.

"Everything's fine."

She didn't say anything immediately, but she was still watching him. He wished she wouldn't. It was giving him very wrong thoughts.

"Are you annoyed with me?" she asked at last as if she'd just figured it out.

He swallowed. He'd been annoyed earlier, but he'd known even then it was irrational. She hadn't done anything wrong. It wasn't her fault she looked so luscious all of a sudden and he couldn't stop thinking about it.

"Jonathan?" she prompted, making him realize yet again he hadn't answered her. "Are you annoyed?"

"No. Of course, not." He tempered his tone so as not to convey his impatience over her pursuing the questioning when he obviously wanted to be left alone.

"You *are* annoyed," she said, as if it was resolved now in her mind. "Or frustrated or something. What did I do?"

"You didn't do anything." If she didn't shut up soon, he was just going to leave the room. He could think of some sort of an excuse.

"Jonathan, look at me," she said sharply.

He did and then knew it was a mistake. She was on her side, propping her head on one hand. Her top had slipped down, exposing far more cleavage than was good for him to see. Too much of her fair skin was exposed, looking smooth and soft and tempting. And her full lips were turned down in a frown.

"Tell me what you're frustrated about."

He obviously couldn't tell her his most urgent frustration, so he hid that with a lesser frustration from earlier, the one he didn't care about anymore. "It's really nothing. I had thought we might do some sightseeing today, just to get away. I wish you would have checked with me before you went shopping."

It sounded petty even as he said it, but it was better than admitting how much he was fighting arousal.

Her lower lip fell open in astonishment. "Are you kidding? I *did* check with you. You said it was fine."

"What could I have said then? You'd already made plans."

She took a deep breath, evidently suppressing a surge of annoyance. "You've got to tell me things, Jonathan. Seriously. We're never going to get through this otherwise. I know you're the strong, silent type or whatever, but this isn't going to work unless you communicate a little more."

"Communicate what?" He was almost relieved at the surge of annoyance since it dampened his physical response. A little.

"Communicate what you want! How am I supposed to know what you're thinking unless you tell me? I can figure a few things out on my own, but not everything and not all the time."

"I tell you what you need to know. The rest of it doesn't matter."

"Of course it matters," she exclaimed, her voice rising in her frustration. "You'd had something in mind for us to do today, but you never told me what it was. I would have been thrilled to go sightseeing with you. It would have been much better than spending endless hours shopping for wedding lingerie for someone else's marriage."

She broke off, flushing deeply, as if she were suddenly embarrassed.

He wasn't sure why she would be embarrassed, but it made her look even more desirable, and he felt his groin tightening again at the sight.

"Anyway, the point is I would have been happy to do what you'd been planning if you'd bothered to let me know what it was!"

"Okay. Fine. I'm sorry," he muttered, unused to seeing Sarah so intense and demanding and unsettled by how irresistible he was finding it.

He was used to her fitting herself around him so smoothly he was barely aware of her a lot of the time. He hadn't realized she was so passionate. About anything.

He wondered if she'd be passionate in bed.

He really shouldn't have wondered that. He was fully aroused now, and he shifted awkwardly, making sure to position himself under the covers in a way that it wouldn't show.

She sighed deeply and seemed to release all her urgency. "I'm sorry," she murmured, "I shouldn't have been... been so snippy. But please try to talk to me a little more. I'm doing my best, but it's hard. I don't want to mess this up."

"You're doing great," he said since she looked momentarily insecure. "I appreciate you doing it at all. Was shopping really so bad?"

"No. It wasn't that bad. I'm just not a shopping kind of person. They were both really nice. Even Laurel, even though at first I thought... Anyway, it was fine. It just got a little weird when they kept wanting me to buy lingerie too."

The image of Sarah in sexy lingerie was one he wished hadn't entered his mind. Then he thought about her in the stockings she was wearing the day before. Tumbled and sleepy as she'd been when he'd woken her up earlier this week.

It took all his self-control not to roll over and kiss her the way he had that morning. That kiss had been spontaneous, just to prove he could act appropriately engaged, but it had felt real in a way it shouldn't.

He wanted to do it again. He wanted to do even more.

He wanted Sarah. Bad.

He turned out the light so he couldn't see her anymore. Then he waited very uncomfortably until her breathing slowed and deepened.

When she was asleep, he got up and went to the bathroom to take care of the inconvenient erection as quickly and quietly as he could.

CHAPTER FOUR

Sarah woke up feeling way too warm and cozy.

She knew immediately something was wrong—she never woke up feeling so good. Shifting a little, she felt something hard and hot beneath her cheek and against her chest and belly. She lifted her head and peered through heavy eyelids to see Jonathan's face just a few inches from hers.

Sucking in a quick breath, she drew back the arm that was wrapped around his waist and rolled over so she wasn't pressed up against his side. Her cheek was hot from being smashed up against his chest.

She must have rolled over to snuggle with him in her sleep, she realized with a wave of embarrassment.

Fortunately, he was still asleep. Or he had been until she jerked away. He looked up at her groggily, his brown eyes disoriented and strangely soft. "Hi," he said.

Despite herself, she couldn't help but smile in response. "Hi." An almost irresistible impulse hit her. She wanted to curl up beside him again, tuck herself beneath his arm, feel him breathe beneath her cheek.

She wanted it so badly it hurt.

But this was Jonathan. Her boss. And she could never have him that way. Even if she didn't work for him, he would never want *her*.

"What time is it?" Jonathan asked. He could have looked over at the clock himself, but he didn't. He was still gazing up at her with sleepy affection.

It wasn't affection. She wasn't so foolish as to believe so. It must just be how he looked when he first woke up.

"Not even five. Too early to get up."

He made a murmured sound of affirmation, and she settled herself under the covers, still fighting the impulse to scoot closer to him. He breathed beside her, slowly, steadily. She could feel the heat from his big body.

She had no idea what he was thinking, what he felt about... anything.

And there wasn't much chance she would ever find out.

~

After breakfast that morning, Jonathan disappeared again, exactly as he had two nights before.

It was honestly a little annoying.

She was his guest here. She was doing him a favor. It was his responsibility to make sure she wasn't deserted to a bunch of intimidating strangers.

The house guests had all scattered for the morning. Marietta and Laurel had gone to the final fitting of the wedding dress. They'd invited Sarah, but she'd politely refused. They were both very friendly, but she didn't know them very well. Wedding dress fittings seemed like something you wouldn't want to do with a stranger.

Besides, Jonathan had mentioned he'd wanted to do some sightseeing with her yesterday, so she thought maybe they could do it today instead.

Except he'd disappeared.

Instead of going up and hiding in her room—which was what she really wanted to do—Sarah walked around the gardens. They were remarkable and must take an army of gardeners to keep so well tended. She wandered aimlessly, finding unexpected nooks and hidden bowers and trying not to brood over Jonathan's frustrating behavior.

As she turned around one long, immaculate hedge, she almost ran into Cyrus Damon. He was walking quickly, his phone in his hand and a frown on his face.

"Oh, I'm sorry," Sarah said instinctively, although the near collision was as much his fault as hers. "I wasn't looking where I was going."

"My fault," he said, his expression changing into a courteous smile. "Can I help you find something?"

"No, no. I was just wandering around, admiring the gardens. I hope that's all right."

"Of course it is, my dear. I hope you're making yourself at home." He glanced behind her, as if he were looking to see if anyone was trailing. "You're on your own this morning?"

The implication in his raised eyebrows was clear. His nephew was failing in his duties.

She swallowed over the temptation to make an excuse for Jonathan. There was no excuse. He was supposed to be her fiancé, and he'd left her alone in a strange place. "Yes, I am." She smiled to make it clear she was content with the situation.

She might just be a fake fiancée, but she wasn't going to be the kind who whined about being neglected.

"Then may I join you?" Cyrus asked, with a formal courtesy she'd rarely encountered.

"Thank you. But you really don't have to. I'm sure you're busy, and I don't mind—"

"I'm not busy at all," he insisted. It was convincing, although it must be a lie. By all accounts, the man had made his fortune by working harder than anyone else. "Have you stumbled upon the secret garden yet?"

"No," she said, charmed by the idea and the girlish daydreams it evoked. "I don't think so. I used to love that book."

He wasn't an attractive man—graying, average-sized, and nondescript. But when he smiled in that winsome way, he transformed into something incredibly appealing. For the first time, she could see the resemblance to Jonathan. "Then you'll love the garden. Let me show you."

They walked slowly, occasionally talking companionably about the flowers, sculptures, and trees they passed. After a few minutes, he asked her about her family, and she told him about her parents' small web-design business in Nevada and about her sister, nephews, and niece, who now lived in the same neighborhood as her parents.

He seemed genuinely interested, although it was a very average, unimpressive family background. There was something faintly wistful in his eyes when he asked if they were all still close.

She told him the truth. She'd always been close to her family. She talked to her parents every day and her sister at least once a week. But then she wished she hadn't told him, since it seemed to have made Cyrus sad.

He didn't reply, and she didn't know what to say. So they walked in silence until they rounded another large ornamental hedge and moved into a wooded area. After a minute, they nearly ran into a stone wall. "Here it is," Cyrus said. "The door is just here. The key is hidden, of course."

"I can see why it's secret," she said when he pushed his way past thick branches to pull out a loose stone and retrieve a key. "I never would have found this on my own."

When he opened the creaky door, she clapped her hands in uninhibited delight. Unlike the rest of the gardens, which were formal and immaculate, this one was free and sprawling in the English style, with flower beds spilling over into each other, big trees growing in haphazard directions, and stone benches and pots nearly overgrown with ivy and vines.

"I love it!" She turned full circle, trying to take in everything. "It's my favorite part of the whole estate."

After a moment, she shot him a quick glance, not wanting her comment to be unintentionally insulting. Cyrus didn't look offended, however. He looked wistful again.

"Was this here when you bought the estate?" she asked, searching for innocuous conversation since she was feeling strangely sorry for the man beside her and had no idea what to do with the feeling.

He nodded. "One of the previous owners built it in the nineteenth century. It was completely overrun when I bought it. My landscapers wanted to just tear the walls down, but I wouldn't let them. It took years to get it back into shape."

"I'm so glad you did. I love it."

She stood a little awkwardly, unsure of whether he would want to leave or not now that he'd shown her the garden. She didn't want to leave yet, but she didn't want him to stick around just to entertain her.

She was trying to think of a polite way to suggest that he could leave her on her own in the garden when he walked over to one of the stone benches. "Would you like to sit?"

She walked over, amazed that he didn't sit until she did. Sarah didn't think anyone followed old rules of courtesy anymore.

Cyrus folded his hands in his lap and stared down at the grass at his feet. "Is Jonathan doing all right?" he asked, without prelude or segue.

Sarah blinked, processing the question and what it might mean. "Yes. He's fine."

"I know he's successful in his career. What I mean is—is he happy?"

"I think he's happy," Sarah said slowly. "I hope he is, anyway."

Cyrus looked at her, almost urgently. "I don't mean the question to be any sort of affront against you. I'm very pleased he's decided to marry and that he's chosen you. But he never talks to me."

"I know he talks on the phone to you fairly often." She had no idea how to handle this conversation. She didn't want to say anything about Jonathan she shouldn't—since she knew he had mixed feelings about his uncle—but Cyrus seemed so inexplicably needy. She wanted to make him feel better.

"But he never says anything—anything *real*. I don't feel like I know him at all, and I've never been able to reach him. I have tried." He looked away again. "I *have* tried."

Sarah swallowed over a thick knot in her throat. There was no reason to feel emotional, but she did. "Jonathan is just that way. He's really private, and he doesn't open up easily."

"How did you do it?" Cyrus shook his head, as if he realized the question was rude and inappropriate. "I'm sorry. If you have any advice for me on how to best reach him, I would appreciate it."

She didn't know much about this man, but she knew enough to realize his asking for help was uncharacteristic and noteworthy. Something must really be bothering him. From what she'd heard, he'd had a big blowup with Harrison last year, which they'd just now gotten past. And until recently, Andrew had a notorious reputation that probably put him on the outs with his uncle as well.

Benjamin, the youngest Damon nephew, didn't talk to any of them. No one knew whether he was going to come to the wedding or not, although his mother was supposed to arrive the following day.

Sarah suddenly wondered if Cyrus Damon might be lonely. He might be a rigid, old-fashioned tyrant, but that didn't mean he couldn't get lonely.

She thought for a minute before she answered, trying to give him the best response she could. "He closes up if you try to force personal topics on him. He'll feel like it's prying and like it's artificial if you haven't built up to it naturally. Maybe you can talk to him about his work. He's passionate about that and he can talk about it all day long. If he knows you're really interested in it, he'll be more likely to believe you want to get to know him."

Damon nodded, his face reflective. "I've talked to him about his work before."

"But it was always in the context of funding the project, right? Maybe you can show interest in the work for its own sake."

After she'd spoken, she thought she'd made a mistake. She cringed inwardly, afraid he would think she'd insulted him.

But he didn't look offended. Just thoughtful still.

"He...," she began, then trailed off when she rethought the comment.

"He what?"

"He *does* things to show how he feels, rather than says things." She knew this was true, and it was one of the reasons she loved him. Jonathan had never once told her he appreciated her as an assistant, but he showed her all the time—by stocking her peppermints, by fixing her chair wheel, by trusting her with really important tasks without any sort of micromanaging.

Since Cyrus didn't respond, she figured the topic was over, so she just sat in silence, admiring the garden, thinking about Jonathan.

After a few minutes, Cyrus said without warning, "His parents were not affectionate."

She turned sharply to look at him. "What?"

"Jonathan's parents. They were not affectionate. At all. Now, I will be the first to admit that I'm not a domestic man and I know next to nothing about raising children. But even I could have done better than his parents—my brother and sister-in-law."

"Were they..." She trailed off, unsure of how much she could presume. He might be in an atypically talkative mood, but that didn't mean he would welcome invasive questions.

"They weren't abusive, of course. I believe they loved him. But they treated him like an adult, even when he was barely past a toddler. They praised him for achievements. They kept pushing him to excel more and more in academics—even when he was just ten. I really think he might have believed they only loved him when he earned it."

Sarah gulped, understanding something about Jonathan she hadn't known before. It fit. It fit perfectly with the rest of what she knew about him—why he only allowed work into his life, why he did things to show he appreciated other people and never wanted any thanks.

And her heart ached for him, more than it ever had before.

Realizing Cyrus was waiting for an answer, she managed to say, "That's too bad."

"It is. I worry about him."

She looked at the man beside her and suddenly wondered if he knew that Jonathan believed Cyrus only cared about him when he earned it too. Jonathan's whole approach to the lab, its funding, and his uncle made sense in a way it hadn't before.

"Is he okay?" Cyrus asked again, with a different resonance this time.

"He's really fine. Everyone who works with him loves him. They really do. He'll always be who he is, but what he is is a really good man. I don't think you need to worry about him."

Cyrus reached over and patted her hand. "I'm glad he has you, my dear. It takes a lot of worries off my mind, knowing he has someone to love him like you."

Sarah couldn't meet his eyes. For the first time, she realized she shouldn't have agreed to this engagement farce. Not because it was making her indulge in hopes about Jonathan that could never come to pass—although it was—but because lying was just plain wrong.

~

Jonathan hadn't had anything to do that morning, so he'd found an empty room and gone through some more of his collected e-mail since working made him feel like he wasn't a complete waste of space.

It also took his mind off how much (and how wrongly) he was thinking about Sarah.

It was almost lunch before he finished up, figuring he'd better find everyone else. He went downstairs and didn't see anyone, so he wandered until he found Gordon.

The butler was on the back patio, where the staff was laying out the table for lunch. Gordon was arranging the centerpiece.

"Hey, Gordon," Jonathan said. "Where is everyone?"

Gordon glanced over but didn't stop clipping and positioning the tulips. "Ms. Edwards and Ms. Gray are on their way back from the dress fitting, and Harrison and Andrew are still talking to the lawyer."

Jonathan frowned. "Didn't Sarah go with Marietta and Laurel?"

"No, sir. She didn't."

"Where is she?"

If Gordon thought it was strange that Jonathan didn't know where his own fiancée was, his expression didn't convey it in the slightest. "When I last saw her a couple of hours ago, she was going to walk in the gardens."

Jonathan's frown deepened. "She's been walking in the garden all this time?" If she hadn't gone with the other women for the dress fitting, why the hell hadn't she come to find him? He would have been happy for the company.

"I'm afraid I don't know, sir. Would you like me to send someone to find her? Or perhaps you'd like to look yourself?" The question was mild, with no accusatory intonation.

But Jonathan knew very well that Gordon thought he should have done a better job taking care of his fiancée and not set her adrift in the vast gardens of the estate by herself.

"I'll go find her," Jonathan murmured, heading off the patio and across the wide lawn that led to the gardens.

The gardens were endless. It might take him an hour to find her. And she might not even still be there.

But he didn't know where else she would be. Gordon would know if she'd come back into the house.

He hadn't even reached the Rococo fountain when he saw Sarah. She looked absolutely beautiful in the noonday sun, the light gilding her red hair and making her skin glow. She wore a casual, flowing skirt and soft top, and the fabric of both clung to her luscious body.

Jonathan stared, wondering how he'd not realized she was so gorgeous all this time.

She was smiling, warm and vivid, up at his uncle.

The sight was disturbing—not just because she was so lovely and desirable, but because she was enjoying his uncle's company so much.

His uncle was obviously enjoying her company too.

They saw him, and Sarah waved. As Jonathan watched, Cyrus Damon lifted her hand and brought it to his lips in an old-fashioned gesture of parting. Then he walked back toward the house at a different angle than the one Jonathan had taken. He gestured to him with a friendly greeting which Jonathan returned.

Jonathan was still standing in the same place when Sarah came up to him.

"What's going on?" he demanded, looking at his uncle's retreating back.

Her full lips turned down. "What do you mean? I was just talking to your uncle. He showed me the secret garden."

"What garden?" He had no idea what she was talking about, and he didn't like that she and his uncle suddenly seemed to be close.

As if she might drift into his uncle's world and no longer be part of his.

He couldn't stand to not have her as part of his world. He didn't know why he hadn't realized it before.

"The walled garden near the woods. He called it the secret garden."

Jonathan shrugged and shook his head. "It doesn't matter. I thought you'd gone with Marietta and Laurel."

"No." Her blue eyes had widened, and they looked startlingly blue in the sunlight. "Why did you think that?"

"Marietta said she'd asked you, so I assumed you'd go."

"Well, I didn't. I thought…" She shook her head slightly, as if changing her mind. "What have you been doing?"

He shrugged again. "Nothing."

"Well, I couldn't find you earlier, so you must have been doing something."

Jonathan wasn't about to tell her he'd been working all morning. She already thought he was incapable of anything but work, and she didn't need to be even less impressed with him than she was. "It doesn't matter. I was around. Why couldn't you find me?"

"What is that supposed to mean?" She'd been on the edge of annoyed before, but now she'd crossed the line. Her cheeks were flushed and her eyes narrowed. "I looked around and didn't see you. Was I supposed to ask Gordon and the rest of the staff to do a full-fledged hunt for my fiancé?"

"Why are you angry?" She was always so even-tempered. This sign of spirit, as arousing as it was, was quite disorienting.

She snapped. He'd never seen it happen before. She got so tense she was shaking with it, and her voice was clipped and cold. "I'm angry because I'm doing you a favor by pretending to be engaged to you, and you act like you want nothing to do with me. I don't know any of these people. They're *your* family. But you keep leaving me alone with them while you go lurk in some dark corner somewhere. It's just *rude*."

Jonathan froze, taking in her words and what they implied. It was rude, he realized. Evidently she wanted his

71

company. She'd prefer to be with him than with anyone else here.

"Well?" she prompted, when he didn't respond. "You don't have anything to say for yourself?"

"Sorry. I wasn't thinking. You seemed to get along with them all so well I just assumed... Sorry."

He felt—and no doubt sounded—like an idiot. And he doubted his inarticulate apology would satisfy her. When he'd dated girls in the past and they'd complained that he was neglecting them for study or work in the lab, it would take hours for them to get over their bad moods.

But Sarah's face and shoulders relaxed immediately. She peered into his face and seemed content with whatever she saw there. "Okay. It's fine. I don't need to be entertained or have company twenty-four hours a day, but it would be nice if you could at least tell me what you're doing so I'll know if I need to make my own plans."

"I will," he said. "Sorry."

"It's fine. I'm not mad or anything." She looked flushed again, but more because she was flustered than because she was angry.

"You *were* mad."

She gave him a quick, quirky smile. "Maybe just a little."

"I've never seen you angry before this week."

"Everyone gets angry occasionally. Even you."

They'd started walking back toward the house instinctively, and Jonathan slanted her a discreet look. He wasn't positive, but she appeared to be teasing him.

"Not very much. It's usually not worth the effort."

"One day," she said, a fond, teasing note in her voice he'd never heard there before, "I'm going to see you totally lose it."

He kind of liked the tone, so he smiled despite himself. "I doubt it."

"I will. One day. And I'm going to totally gloat when you do."

He laughed. He couldn't help it. At the moment, he couldn't imagine what would possibly get him so angry, so he could say in all truthfulness, "I doubt you'll ever have the opportunity, but if I lose it one day, you'll deserve to gloat."

~

That evening after dinner, Jonathan went back up to the media room to play Sea and Sky.

He'd checked to see that Sarah was occupied. She was tying up little sacks of birdseed with Laurel to throw at the newlyweds instead of rice as they were leaving. Harrison was working on e-mail, and Andrew was talking to their uncle about the inn he and Laurel managed in Santorini.

Since everyone else was occupied, Jonathan figured he was free to do what he wanted.

He'd been playing for about an hour when he was conscious of a presence behind him.

Reluctantly, he turned to see Sarah standing in the doorway, staring at him with narrowed eyes.

"So this is what you've been doing when you sneak away," she said.

He gave her a sheepish shrug. "Nothing else to do."

"Isn't this game like twenty years old?"

"I used to play it as a kid when I was here on holiday. I can't believe my uncle still has it."

She came over to sit beside him on the floor, leaning back against the couch just as he was. He'd taken off the jacket and tie he'd worn for dinner, but she still wore a long gray skirt with a very high slit on one side and a blue silk top that matched her eyes. She seemed unconscious of her nice clothes though as she picked up a second joystick. "How do you play?"

He'd expected her to mock him. She seemed to be serious, however, gazing up at him and waiting for instructions.

He felt the strangest overflow of feeling, a tension in his chest, in his stomach. He'd never met anyone like her, never realized anyone could know him as well as she did and still want to be around him when it wasn't even part of her job, even when he was unquestionably unimpressive.

"Jonathan?" she prompted, her expression becoming slightly confused.

"Yeah," he said, shaking himself out of the weird thought. "It's not hard. You can pick it up quickly. The object is to collect stars and starfish while not getting hit with birds and fish."

She did pick it up quickly. She was smart and coordinated, and in twenty minutes she could provide him with a decent challenge. They played for two hours, focused intently on the game, more and more competitive as she kept getting closer to beating him.

She didn't beat him. No one ever had. But she came surprisingly close a few times. There was something intoxicating about it, about how she laughed, about how intensely she focused, about how excited she became when she did well.

"All right," she said at last, setting down her joystick after just missing out on a win. "I give up for tonight. We'll try again later though, so don't get too comfortable."

He wasn't comfortable. His back hurt a little from sitting too long on the floor like this, and he was now having trouble not leering at her legs. She'd evidently forgotten she was wearing a dress, and one of her legs was fully visible through the high slit.

She was wearing another pair of those irresistible lace-topped stockings. He could see where the lace met her skin.

She noticed his distraction and got flustered when she saw how much leg she was exposing. "Sorry," she mumbled, adjusting her skirt and tucking her leg back under it. "I'm not used to wearing clothes like this."

He wasn't used to seeing her in clothes like that, but he realized she'd always been beautiful. Even in less revealing clothes and with her hair pulled back in a ponytail, she hadn't looked that much different.

He'd just never been conscious of it before.

He was very much afraid that he would never see her as anything but gorgeous from now on. Even back in the lab, in her white lab coat and no-nonsense work mood, he'd still want her this intensely.

It was a very disturbing thought.

She still seemed embarrassed—either at her inadvertent exposure or at the way he was staring at her—as she got to her feet. "I think I'm going to go to bed."

"Yeah," he said, glancing at his watch. "I guess it's pretty late."

They went down to their room. He took a shower since he was slightly aroused and it wouldn't be smart to go to bed with her in that condition. By the time he came out, she was under the covers and had turned off all but the light on his side of the bed.

They didn't talk as he got in bed and turned off the light. It was earlier than he normally went to sleep, but he didn't feel like reading.

They lay awake in silence for several minutes. She was perfectly still beside him, but he knew she was awake.

Finally, she said what she'd obviously been thinking about. "Your uncle is worried about you."

He tensed slightly, not minding talking to her but not liking the direction of the conversation. "What do you mean?"

"He's worried about you. He was asking me about you today in the garden. He wanted to make sure you were happy."

"What did you tell him?"

"I told him you were."

He relaxed slightly.

"He loves you, you know." Her voice was mild, almost casual. "He wants to connect with you but doesn't know how."

Jonathan didn't say anything. Had no idea what to say, even if he'd wanted to.

"I know you think he doesn't care much about you, but he does. I think if you made a little effort to connect with him, it would pay off."

A thick bubble of feeling and confusion choked him. He had no idea how Sarah had known that about him. He didn't like that she knew. It made him feel vulnerable.

As vulnerable as the idea that his uncle wanted to connect with him. He'd never believed that was true. Still couldn't really believe it. He'd never been able to do anything to really impress his uncle. Even his work at the lab wasn't enough.

"Jonathan?" Sarah prompted finally.

"Yeah," he muttered. "It's not really any of your business."

"Okay. Sorry."

He'd said the worst possible thing he could have said. He'd hurt her feelings. He could hear it in her voice, sense it in the tension of her body beside his. She'd been trying to help him, and he'd thrown it back into her face.

He was an idiot and an ass in almost every way. "I'm sorry," he said, "I didn't mean to—"

"No, it's fine. I understand. I shouldn't pry."

Her voice was natural again, but he thought she was still upset.

"Good night," she added, ending the conversation by rolling over so she was facing away from him on the bed.

Jonathan wanted to say something, wanted to make it better. He wanted her to look at him the way she'd been looking at him earlier that evening—like he was something special.

He wished he was like Harrison or Andrew, always able to find the right words.

But he couldn't. He didn't know how to fix it. So he just said "good night" back to her and rolled over away from her, counting down the days until this trip was over and his life could return to normal again.

Jonathan wasn't sure how it happened.

He wasn't conscious of having an erotic dream, but the first thing he was aware of on awakening was being deeply, dangerously aroused.

It wasn't like a normal morning hard-on either. The need was urgent, and it was the only thing in the world he was aware of.

Then he became conscious of a few more things, which only deepened his arousal. He must have moved in his sleep because he was almost on top of a soft, warm, female body.

She was wearing some sort of tank top to sleep in, but it had somehow gotten pushed up, so his bare chest pressed against the smooth, bare skin of her back.

Her hair was all around, soft and fragrant, in his face, against his skin. He shifted since even in his half-awakened state, he knew he shouldn't be lying on top of someone.

He was too heavy.

She moaned when he moved, and the throaty sound went straight to his groin. She pushed her bottom up as he shifted until it was in perfect, torturous alignment with his erection.

She was still asleep, he realized. She made a huff of sound and pressed her hips up again, as if she were instinctively seeking what she'd felt before.

No wonder he'd woken up so turned on. She was clearly having a sexy dream, and it felt all too real to him.

He couldn't seem to think. Couldn't seem to focus. The world had reduced to a hot haze of need, and nothing mattered but the feel of this woman and the throbbing need of his body.

He pushed back against her ass, letting out a breath at the delicious pressure where he desperately needed it.

She moaned and pushed up against his thrust.

Sarah. He wanted Sarah so much.

Some faint hint of awareness prodded its way into his muddled mind, telling him he couldn't hump a sleeping woman no matter how desperately he needed to.

With great effort, he started to roll over.

As soon as he lifted his weight from her, she whimpered in protest and raised her hips again. "No, no," she mumbled, her cheek pressed against the pillow and her eyes still closed. "Don't stop. I want it. Please. I want it."

She was awake now, he realized. Whether she was before or not, he didn't know. He also didn't know *how* awake she was. She was obviously aroused, but she might not even be conscious of who he was.

If she was awake, she wasn't likely to want *him*.

"Jonathan, please," she breathed. "I want you. Please." Her hands fumbled until she was clutching the sheet beneath her with both hands.

He groaned low in his throat, barely audible, as he rolled over her again, moving into the same position. If she wanted this, wanted him, there was no way he'd be able to stop himself.

He pressed his groin into her soft, round ass, just as she was pressing it up toward him. They both huffed in pleasure. Then they did it again.

A clumsy, half-asleep dry hump wasn't exactly what he would have chosen, but he needed something, he needed *her*. And he would take what he could get.

Then Sarah started shifting awkwardly beneath him, and he realized she was trying to take off her little cotton shorts. He helped her, which was only polite.

At least, that was what his fuzzy brain told him.

"Jonathan," she whimpered, lifting her now bare bottom toward him again. "Please, please."

He reached down to feel her intimately, taking a few moments in his uncoordinated state to find and ascertain that she was really aroused, really wet. Then he smothered a groan, pulled his erection free of his underwear, and raised her bottom a little more so he could align himself at her entrance.

"Yes, yes, I want it. Just like that." She was still mostly on her stomach, with just her butt in the air, and he'd never wanted anyone more.

He straddled her hips and pushed into her slowly, groaning silently at the intense pleasure of being enveloped by her hot, clinging channel. She moaned uninhibitedly as he maneuvered his way in, as if it felt just as good to her.

He loved how much she seemed to want him, as if she couldn't possibly hold back her response.

When he began to thrust, it was in short, tight pumps by necessity, their position allowing nothing else. But she huffed in pleasure on each instroke, her hands scrambling for purchase in the bedding and her bottom eagerly rocking up to meet his thrusts.

His whole body was so tense he was shaking with it, and he was vaguely conscious of the fact that he shouldn't be doing this—he shouldn't be fucking Sarah this way, half-asleep and without discussion or preparation. But he couldn't help it. She obviously wanted it, and he couldn't summon any sort of reasonable restraint.

He braced himself on both arms above her, working his erection inside her in a way that produced the kind of agonizing friction he needed. He wasn't sure how long it lasted—the urgent tangle of hot bodies, damp flesh, accelerating breath, and soft moans and whimpers from Sarah.

Then her body tightened dramatically and she gasped, "Oh, God, oh, God, I'm gonna come."

His motion intensified as he thrust into her from behind, fast and hard. Then her body clamped down around the orgasm, and she cried out in breathy pleasure as she shook and shuddered beneath him.

"Jonathan," she rasped against the pillow. "So good. So good."

He kept thrusting even as she came down, too far gone to hold back his primitive need to claim her in any way he could, and soon she cried, "Oh God! Again!" as her body tightened up once more.

She made a helpless sobbing sound as she came the second time, letting herself go to the pleasure without any restraint.

She gasped out his name again as she came down, and her body started to soften. He loved how she said it with a catch in the middle, as if she were too overcome to speak. "Jon-athan. Jon-athan."

He had almost come with her the second time, only the idea of this ending and his having to deal with the implications holding back the thread of his control.

He didn't want this to end. Not yet.

He didn't know what he would do when it was over.

CHAPTER FIVE

Sarah had never come during intercourse before—not once. It wasn't that she couldn't come at all, but it had always been either from oral or manual pleasuring before or after the main event. So, even if she had been in a thinking state, she never would have expected to come the way she had. Twice.

She was dazed and relaxed—and just starting to get self-conscious in her ungainly position—when Jonathan pulled out and rearranged her body so she was on her back beneath him. She parted her legs to make room for him, bending up her knees and pulling his upper body down farther.

Much more comfortable, she sighed in pleasure when he nudged at her entrance and then slid himself in again. She was tighter around him now that she'd come.

Jonathan made a breathy sound. It might have been her name said on an exhale. Then he started to move over her, inside her, against her. She made a silly sound in her throat as the friction triggered delicious sensations.

Part of her knew this was crazy, knew she shouldn't let him do this to her, knew it might be good at the moment but it was going to be really hard to get over. But that part of her was silenced by the roar of need and feeling that overwhelmed her.

She knew she was awake, but it didn't feel like she was awake.

Sarah Stratford, awake in her right mind, didn't do things like this. She didn't have sex with Jonathan Damon in the middle of the night with wild, uninhibited passion.

The fact that she was—she *was*—made the whole thing even hotter. Jonathan was bracing himself on straightened arms, little more than a dark shadow above her in the unlit room. But she knew he was looking down on her, knew the intent focus of his expression, in his eyes.

He made love the way he did everything else, with absolute focus and instinct and skill.

His hips were working urgently, and heat radiated off his body in waves. His breathing was fast and raspy, but otherwise he didn't make any sounds.

She rocked up to meet his thrusts, the beginnings of thinking awareness swallowed up again in the wave of pleasure and need.

He wasn't a selfish lover or even a slightly thoughtless one like Matt had been, trying for a while but then eventually chasing his own satisfaction. Jonathan was aware of her the whole time, recognizing what she wanted, what she needed, and giving it to her without hesitation. When she clutched at his ass, desperately wanting him to accelerate his steady thrusts, he did. When she squeezed her fingers down to rub her clit, the intense pressure of the pleasure becoming almost torturous, he adjusted to make room for her hand.

She moaned as she rubbed herself, the added sensations pushing her over the plateau.

"Yes." She heard herself panting. "So good, Jonathan. So good. Faster."

He thrust into her faster, and she bent up her knees as she felt another orgasm building inside her. She gave a helpless sob as it finally broke, slamming into her in rhythmic waves. She clawed his shoulders with her fingernails, trying to hold on as she rode out the pleasure with her hips.

"Jon-athan," she gasped when the intensity started to fade and a delicious relaxation took its place. Her body felt almost limp as the tightened muscles let go. "So good. So good."

He grunted, evidently in response to her words. But he was still hard inside her, and she couldn't help but wonder if he was always such a stallion or if he was making a special effort for her.

"Now it's your turn," she said, surprised when her voice was slightly cracked. She reached up and pulled him down into a kiss before she had a chance to think about whether it was a good idea.

They hadn't kissed earlier, just woke up fully aroused and started going at it. She had no idea if he even wanted to kiss her.

He responded though. Immediately. His mouth moved against hers skillfully, eagerly, and she opened so his tongue could slip inside and tangle with hers. His hips started to rock as they kissed, easing into a gentle rhythm that matched the rhythm of his tongue.

Then he broke off the kiss without warning, turning his head to the side and gasping loudly.

She couldn't see his face clearly, she couldn't see his eyes at all, but she knew he was trying to hold back.

She reached up and took his face in both of her hands, his bristles deliciously scratchy against her palms. "You've given me enough," she said. "I want you to take what you want now."

She didn't know if her words worked or if he was just too far gone. But he let out a smothered sound and pushed one of her knees up toward her shoulder, stretching her out farther and allowing him to sink more deeply inside her.

They both moaned at the resulting sensations.

He held her in that position as he started to move. He was too deep to really thrust, but he pushed into her. His whole body was clenched up like a fist, so tight he was almost shaking with it. And his breathing was ragged and loud in the otherwise quiet room.

Sarah tried to process all the sensations, but they were too deep, too strong, too much, too aching. It was mostly pleasure even though she was never going to be able to come like this. She didn't even want to.

"That's right, that's good," she kept gasping as he rocked both of their bodies with the force of his thrusts. "That's good, yes, please, take what you want."

She could feel as he got closer to climax. He fell out of rhythm and his panting turned into soft grunts. Her chest ached with emotion that almost matched the feeling in her body as he finally took what he needed.

He didn't cry out like she had, just made a half-suppressed sound in his throat. But she knew he'd come hard. He shuddered above her as it overtook him, and then he collapsed on top of her, dragging in thick gasps of air against her neck.

He was heavy. And very hot. And she didn't know if she was feeling his sweat or hers.

She didn't care.

Her body was sated, relaxed. And her heart felt even better. Because she knew she'd given Jonathan something, something he hadn't been able to get in another way.

He'd needed her, and she'd met that need. And he'd given her something back.

And it was so good.

He didn't move immediately. She could feel him softening until he slipped out of her body. Then it was really wet.

They hadn't used a condom.

They hadn't intended to do this at all.

She could feel a soreness now since he'd been inside her deep. And he felt even heavier than before. His breathing had slowed, but it wasn't steady yet. His face was buried in her hair.

It was two o'clock in the morning, and Sarah had just made love to her boss.

It felt kind of like she needed to go the bathroom, but she didn't want to move, didn't want him to roll off her, didn't want to lose his weight, the texture of his hair and skin.

She wanted to do it again.

She wanted him—in a way she never should.

But he'd needed her too. She was sure of it.

And that was something.

* * *

Jonathan was so wiped out from sex with Sarah that he fell asleep before he realized it.

He hadn't intended to. He never should have given in to desire, but he had—and it seemed rude to go to sleep before they'd had a chance to talk about it and get things sorted out.

So he'd been trying to get himself together—get his mind to work with something other than the blurry fog of satisfaction and relief and to find some appropriate words to say—but he fell asleep instead.

Sarah must have fallen asleep too, since when he woke up she was still beside him, naked except for the little tank top she still wore. She was curled up next to him, her hair in her face and one of her arms draped over his belly.

He liked how it felt there.

But it was morning now—not the blurry darkness of the night. The room was lit by the sunlight peeking in around the drapes, and he could see her clearly.

He hadn't been able to see her very well last night. Just feel her. But he'd known even by touch that her body was the most sensuous, beautiful thing he'd ever experienced.

He hadn't been wrong. The sheet had slipped down to her hips, and he could clearly see the lush curves and dips of her form. She was so soft, made for touching. And even now, he could barely resist.

She was still sound asleep, her lashes spread out against her skin. She nestled against him more closely, as if she were getting cold.

Automatically, he reached down to pull up the sheet and coverlet over her. Before he did, he was distracted by the most enchanting curve—the graceful dip at the small of her back, just as it curved up into her bottom. Despite how hard he'd come a few hours earlier, his body took interest in that spot.

Her skin was pale. Pale and perfect. A delicate contrast to the vibrancy of her hair.

He pulled up the covers, hiding her from his sight.

It wouldn't do to get fully aroused again since he wouldn't be able to do anything about it.

Covering her up didn't do much good though. He could still feel her. Her breasts were pressed up against his side, and her arm still clung to him as if she didn't want to let him go even in her sleep.

After a few minutes, when no amount of mental lecturing could dampen his arousal, he pulled out from under her arm and climbed out of the bed.

He went immediately to take a shower, trying to rinse off the feel, the smell, the taste of her. Knowing she was still mostly naked in bed, if he couldn't wash her off him, he wouldn't have a chance of getting out of the room without taking her again.

It was a much longer shower than usual by the time he felt recovered and more like himself. He shaved while he was in the bathroom and then put on one of the bathrobes provided in the guestrooms since he hadn't thought to bring any clothes into the bathroom with him.

Sarah was awake when he came back into the room. She'd pulled her pajama shorts back on and was sitting on the side of the bed, her arms crossed over her belly.

Her hair was a tousled mess, and her eyelids heavier than normal, making her look even sexier than she usually did.

But her face was sober, and her eyes were worried as she looked up at him.

He went over to sit beside her on the bed.

He wanted to ask her how she felt, whether she was all right, whether he'd ruined everything by giving into lust in the dark of the night.

What he said was, "We should have used a condom."

She swallowed and glanced away from him. "Yeah."

He'd said the wrong thing as he always did. He knew he had. He couldn't tell if she was annoyed or hurt, but something was wrong. He felt awful—like a selfish ass—and he needed to know if she was all right. "Are you..." His voice broke since he felt so concerned.

Before he could continue, she'd turned back. "I'm on birth control. I just never went off it after Matt and I broke up. So we're all right on that front. And I haven't slept with anyone since Matt. So as long as you're..." She trailed off.

"I'm healthy," he said. He hadn't had sex in longer than she had, but he didn't say it. He still wanted to know if she was all right, but that part of the conversation seemed to have passed.

He just wasn't any good at this.

"What do you..." She glanced down at her hands, which were twisting in her lap now. "What do you think we should do? About this?" She glanced back toward the bed as if she needed to explain what "this" was.

He knew very well what "this" was.

Still feeling guilty and confused and strangely terrified, he began, "I shouldn't have... I should have stopped us."

"I was awake too. As much as you were. We just weren't thinking." Her head was lowered now, her hair shielding her face from his view. It frustrated him since he couldn't tell how she was feeling.

She'd sounded natural and casual enough. Maybe she was.

He sat in silence and stared at the soft waves of her hair. He wanted this to be over. He wanted it to have never happened. He wanted to be back in his lab with a Sarah he knew and trusted, a Sarah that didn't make him feel things he'd never felt.

She finally looked up at him, her blue eyes searching his face. "We can just call it one of those things. A fluke. We can pretend it never happened. If you want." Her voice lifted slightly at the end, making the words a question.

It was exactly what he wanted. She didn't seem hurt or disappointed. She was obviously not nursing a secret passion for him. It would be so much easier than trying to sort through everything he was feeling and make some kind of sense of it.

They could go back to work, and he could find ways to try to make up for his lapse.

"Okay." Then, because he was still worried, he added, "If you're sure. Everything is all right between us?"

"Sure," she said with a smile that was strangely bright. "I'm not about to claim this ring is for real or anything, if that's what you're worried about."

That wasn't what he was worried about. He was worried about hurting her, but she wasn't acting hurt. So he gave her a half smile. "It never crossed my mind."

"All right," she said, "If we've got that taken care of, I'm going to take a shower." When she stood up, one of her legs buckled, and she had to brace herself on the nightstand.

He stood up quickly to support her, reaching out in concern.

"I'm fine," she assured him, pulling gently away from his arm. "Just a little sore." She flashed him a smile as she limped toward the bathroom. "Not that anything happened last night."

~

Sarah cried a little bit in the shower, but she did so quietly and not for very long.

It had been ridiculous for her to hope for anything else to happen. Jonathan was never going to want her for any more than a night. In the light of day, she was what she'd always been—his less-than-beautiful assistant. Smart and helpful but not particularly desirable in any way.

Jonathan would want so much more.

Men just didn't fall for her. She'd dated some in college and grad school, but mostly because she was one of the few women in her programs. Guys didn't seem to really fall for her. Even Matt—whom she'd dated longer than anyone else—had never said he loved her.

She was pretty sure he never had.

It was fine. She had plenty of other things going for her. She just had to make sure this thing didn't threaten her job, so she couldn't let Jonathan see she was hurt or upset about what had happened.

She'd talked herself down from being crushed by the time she finished the shower. And by the time she'd dried her hair and got dressed, she felt ready to face the world.

Nothing had changed. She and Jonathan still worked together, and they would still get along just fine. She'd just had a few good orgasms last night. She wasn't about to complain.

He was already downstairs for breakfast, so she went down to the breakfast room. Harrison, Laurel, and Marietta were at the table too, Marietta laughing at something Harrison had said.

Sarah smiled at everyone and went to get some coffee and fill her plate. She wasn't very hungry, but she didn't want to act like anything was different this morning.

She sat down, asking for details on the tennis match they were talking about. Jonathan hadn't said anything, but she could feel him looking at her closely.

The knowledge was disturbing, and she didn't want him to know she was even slightly disappointed. If he thought she'd be distracted at work from now on, then he might wonder if she could still do her job. So she smiled at him. She smiled at everyone. She laughed when appropriate, and she ate most of her eggs, bacon, and danish.

And soon it felt like her face was going to break in half.

But she made it through breakfast. And she made it through the morning, mostly by accepting Laurel's invitation to help her set up and decorate for the wedding shower she was throwing for Marietta the next day.

Laurel was nicer than Sarah had thought at first. She had an organized, no-nonsense approach to everything— particularly planning something like a wedding—and Sarah couldn't help but admire her clear thinking and efficiency. But she wasn't really brusque, and she seemed to genuinely like and respect Sarah. So Sarah was feeling better by lunchtime, having convinced herself that nothing about her life had really changed.

When she and Laurel walked into the entry hall, Sarah knew immediately that *something* had changed. There were voices coming from the parlor, but the vibes somehow felt all wrong.

She found out why when they followed the voices into the parlor.

Benjamin Damon, the rebel nephew of the family, had decided to come after all.

CHAPTER SIX

Benjamin didn't look anything like a Damon.

He wasn't clean-cut and well dressed like Harrison and Andrew or even handsome in wrinkled clothes like Jonathan. His face was barely visible beneath an untrimmed full beard, and he wore beat-up jeans and had tattoos all over one arm.

He couldn't have showed up in a way more sure to offend his uncle if he'd tried. For all Sarah knew, he *had* been trying.

He'd arrived with a middle-aged, comfortable-looking woman who must be his mother, and he clearly wasn't enthusiastic about being here at all.

When Sarah and Laurel arrived in the parlor, they were introduced to Benjamin and his mother, Lucy Damon.

Sarah wondered if she'd never been married or if she'd reverted to her maiden name after a divorce. She could asked Jonathan later.

The parlor was crowded, with Andrew and Harrison trying to make conversation with Benjamin and Cyrus and Marietta talking to Mrs. Damon.

Jonathan had been listening to his cousins' conversation, but he stood up when Sarah entered the room. She walked over to stand beside him since they were supposed to be engaged.

She felt nervous and kind of upset though, the sight of his big hands, wrinkled shirt, and dark brown eyes making her think about how much she wanted him.

They sat down together on the antique settee he'd been sitting on before, and they were so close their thighs pressed together.

She wondered if he was as uncomfortable as she was or if he was oblivious about the whole thing.

With Jonathan, it was hard to tell.

Harrison was valiantly trying to make civil conversation about Benjamin's work at an architecture firm, but Benjamin's answers were terse and uninformative. When Harrison made an optimistic comment about Benjamin's future, suggesting he would climb the ladder of promotion quickly, Benjamin said bluntly it wasn't going to happen.

Harrison was evidently at a loss, and he looked discreetly to Andrew for help.

Andrew, looking half-annoyed and half-amused, started telling Benjamin about the inn he and Laurel had on Santorini. It was the right move since it allowed him to do most of the talking and the rest of them could join in on mostly natural conversation.

Sarah listened with half her mind, and with other she studied Benjamin. She didn't find him attractive, and she thought he was rather rude, but after a few minutes she decided his behavior wasn't the sulking of a rebellious adolescent. He was grown-up—definitely all man—and he didn't appear petty or mean-spirited.

Rather, she decided he looked trapped, like he was desperate to get away and pulling into his shell was the only way he could make it through the encounter.

She couldn't help but wonder what had happened to make him hate his family so much.

She must not have done a very good job about being discreet in her scrutiny. Benjamin kept catching her eye, and on about the fourth time, he arched his eyebrows and gave her a dry half smile.

She glanced away, hiding a smile. For the first time, she could see that he might actually be as attractive as all the Damon nephews were known to be.

Not as handsome as Jonathan, but she didn't know anyone who was.

She looked up at Jonathan and saw to her surprise that he was watching her. She smiled up at him, a little hesitantly. She really wanted things to get back to normal between them, even if her own emotions were running completely out of control.

He smiled back—the real smile she didn't often see—and she felt a flush of pleasure wash over her.

Maybe everything wasn't messed up. They'd always gotten along so well, and their work could remain the priority.

Unfortunately, their shared look had made her more conscious than ever of his big, warm body beside her. She wanted to lean into him, wanted his arm around her.

To distract herself, she looked at Benjamin again, trying to figure out what the tattoo was that covered one of his inner arms.

Her eyes darted up to his face, and she saw he'd caught her staring again.

Conversation had shifted over to the wedding, and the talk felt disconnected enough for her to start her own conversation. So she covered her staring by explaining to Benjamin quietly, "I was trying to figure out your tattoo."

His eyes were very dark brown above his dark beard, but they weren't cold or unkind. He stretched out his arm so she could see the tattoo better.

It was made up of interconnected shapes that didn't form any coherent pattern. She lowered her brows. "What does it mean?"

"That's what everyone asks."

She frowned, since she'd really wanted to know and didn't appreciate this indirection, but after a moment she could see he wasn't going to tell her.

She rolled her eyes when he gave her another half smile. This smile didn't quite reach his eyes.

To her surprise, Jonathan moved just then, sliding one of his arms around her back and pulling her against his side.

They were supposed to be engaged. He was probably just playing the role. But it seemed strange to Sarah, so she looked up at him.

To most people, he would appear just as laid-back as always, but to her he looked annoyed for some reason.

She had no idea why.

She liked how his arm felt around her. Liked it so much she wanted to pull away. She didn't, of course. They'd gone too far for her to retreat from her role now.

Gordon appeared in the room to tell them lunch was ready, and Sarah sighed in relief as she got up.

Her back, shoulder, and side felt too warm, as if she could still feel Jonathan against her. She couldn't believe she'd had sex with him last night, that he'd made her come so hard, that she'd urged him so shamelessly to take what he wanted.

Nothing was supposed to change, but her life still felt very different than it had been just a week ago.

~

After lunch, the nonfamily wedding guests started to arrive, so the house became hectic and full of conversation. Jonathan said his uncle would be annoyed if he didn't help greet the new guests, but that she didn't have to stick around to help.

She hung around for a while, not wanting to look rude, but after an hour it was clear that she was doing no good. She didn't know anyone, wasn't a member of the family, and couldn't help at all in greeting or making guests feel at home.

So she decided it was safe to slip away.

She took her e-reader and went to the garden, deciding she would read for the afternoon until all the new guests were settled.

She wandered around, trying to find a private nook. Then she remembered the secret garden and made her way to the wall, where she found the hidden key and opened the door.

She settled herself on the hammock and read for a while. Then she actually dozed off.

It was after five when she woke up and realized she should probably get back to the house. She hurriedly locked the door and made her way through the lawns, hedges, and flower beds.

She wasn't late, she told herself. She had plenty of time to dress before dinner. She just felt discombobulated since she'd fallen asleep without intending to.

She ran into Benjamin as she was turning the corner around a hedge. He sat on a bench, reading from an e-reader too.

"We had the same idea, I guess," she said when he looked up and saw her. She showed him hers.

"I don't know what you're thinking in marrying into this family." His words were bitter, and so was his look as he glanced back toward the big manor house.

She sat down beside him, since it seemed rude to walk away or hover over him. "Everyone has been very nice to me."

"Oh, they're always nice."

She studied him closely, trying to figure out why he was so angry. No one had been anything but kind to him since he'd arrived. In fact, they'd run in circles trying to make him feel at home.

"What did they do to you?" she asked bluntly, since he seemed to prefer the direct approach and she really wanted to know.

Benjamin stared out at the statue of a Greek god that perched above a spill of petunias. He didn't answer for a long time.

Then he murmured, "It's not what they did."

Sarah wanted to follow up, but she could see it would be a futile effort. She was a stranger, and he was obviously not the sharing kind.

"Benjamin," she began, basically just stalling as she tried to figure out what to say.

"I actually prefer Ben."

"Oh. Sorry. Ben." No one else called him Ben, but she was happy to call him whatever he wanted. "What are you reading?"

It was an awkward segue, but it turned out to be a good one. They talked about books, and he seemed much more natural and comfortable. Not friendly and certainly not loquacious. But at least she wasn't having to carry the whole conservation.

It was time to dress for dinner when they finally walked back to the house together. And she felt like she'd done a good job in being nice to him and helping him feel more comfortable.

It would be easier for Cyrus—for everyone—if Ben didn't feel like such an outsider, and she was glad she was able to help a little.

She was satisfied with her afternoon's work as she went back to her room. Jonathan was already dressed for dinner in a dark suit and only slightly wrinkled gray dress shirt, and he was sitting on the chaise at the window, reading a journal. He had a comic book next to him, for when he finished the journal or got bored.

He looked at her when she entered but didn't smile.

"Is everything all right?" she asked, since it wasn't his typical expression. "Am I late?"

He glanced at his watch, as if he had no idea what time it was. "What were you doing?"

"Just reading in the garden." She went to the closet and tried to figure out what she should wear. She already had outfits picked out for the wedding shower, the rehearsal dinner, and the wedding itself—but it was hard to have to look nice every single evening. Pretty soon, she would have to start repeating outfits.

"What were you reading?" he asked.

"Nothing too interesting," she replied, not wanting to tell him she was reading the latest of a very sexy vampire series. His image of her didn't include vampires or sexy books, and she'd like for it to remain that way.

She pulled out a blue silk sheath dress—the first one the attendant had suggested she try on at the department store. She hadn't worn it yet, since it was more revealing than the other dresses she'd worn so far and she was a little nervous about it.

But she decided she'd be brave, so she hung it over one arm. When she turned, she saw Jonathan was watching her.

"You spent all afternoon reading something not interesting?"

She'd almost forgotten her innocuous comment, and she was a little annoyed he was pursuing this random conversation. "It was fine. Just a book. Nothing you would have heard of. Why does it matter?"

"It doesn't."

She went to the drawer and picked out a pair of stockings. Then decided she had better wear a different pair of underwear or she'd have a panty line visible beneath the thin fabric of her dress. So she grabbed a lace thong, very different from the cotton bikini panties in different bright colors she normally wore.

She hid the stockings and the panties beneath her dress since Jonathan was still sitting there watching her.

It would have been polite for him to leave and let her dress in privacy, but he didn't.

"How do you know I wouldn't have heard of it?" he asked.

She frowned. "You read scientific journals and comic books. It wasn't one of those."

Why the hell had he gotten the book she was reading between his teeth this way? He could be obnoxiously stubborn when he got a hold of something.

Since he didn't appear inclined to leave, she went into the bathroom to change. She was about to close the door when he said, "I do occasionally read other things, you know."

There was the overly patient note in his tone that she'd heard before when he was annoyed by something. She couldn't for the life of her figure out what would have annoyed him. She left the door half-open while she stripped off her top and pants. "It wasn't an insult. I just never see you reading anything else."

He didn't answer, so to change the direction of the conversation, she said, "I ran into Ben as I was coming back. He's really interesting."

"Is he?"

The tense note was even stronger now in his voice, so her attempt at misdirection hadn't worked.

She peeled off her panties and pulled on the lace thong, wondering how women wore this kind of sexy underwear all the time. She felt weird and uncomfortable in it, but at least it would save her from having a panty line.

She sat down to pull on her stockings. Those she was starting to like. They made her feel sensual and old-fashioned, something she almost never felt.

"What happened with him?" she asked through the half-open door. "With Ben, I mean. Why is he so down on the family?"

She stood up and caught a glimpse of herself in the mirror. Her hair needed brushing, she needed to put on lipstick, and her curves were a little too curvy. But still, she was surprised by how pretty and sexy she looked in the underwear.

She'd never had that experience looking in a mirror before.

"What does it matter?" Jonathan asked from the bedroom.

She was so distracted by looking at herself that she'd lost the thread of the conversation. "What?"

She unzipped the dress and stepped into it, sliding it up over her body.

"Why does it matter why Benjamin is angry at all of us?"

"I guess it doesn't." She didn't know why Jonathan was in such a bad mood, but it was starting to get on her nerves. "I was just curious. No need to snap my head off."

She tried to contort herself to zip the dress up the back, but it was so snugly fitted that she was afraid she might rip a seam. So she came out with it unzipped.

She was about to ask for help when she saw what Jonathan was doing.

He was looking at her e-reader.

"Hey! That's private!" She ran over to him and tried to snatch the e-reader out of his hands.

He easily eluded her hands. "You wouldn't tell me what you were reading," he said as if that were some sort of justification.

She shook with indignation and made another lunge for her e-reader. She ended up tackling him, and they both landed in a tumble on the bed.

"That's mine," she raged. "You don't get to just go in and read it." She kept grabbing for the little device, and she finally managed to get her hands on it. "It's an invasion of privacy."

"Sorry," he said. His tone had changed now, and it sounded warm, like he wanted to laugh. "You wouldn't tell me what you were reading."

"That's not an excuse." She tried to sit up since she was sprawled out inelegantly on top of him. She was suddenly aware that he was big and alive and masculine and on the bed.

"Evidently," he murmured, his dark eyes softer than she'd expected, "you like to read about vampires having very kinky sex."

She flushed hotly and tried to push herself up, her hands braced on his broad shoulders. "That's none of your business. They're very popular books."

His hands had settled on her waist as if he were going to help her up. But he didn't. "I guess a lot of people like to read about vampires having very kinky sex."

"There's a lot more to the books than the sex," she explained, strangely mesmerized by the look in his eyes.

It looked almost like he was going to kiss her.

He'd kissed her last night, on this very bed. She'd kissed him. She wanted to do it again.

But, no, she was wrong about him again. He hadn't been thinking about kissing her. He lifted his eyebrows and asked, "Why is your dress hanging open?"

She sucked in a surprised breath and climbed off him, her cheeks burning with new embarrassment and her chest aching slightly in disappointment.

She really needed to stop expecting something good to happen between them. It was never going to happen.

"I needed help with the zipper," she explained, turning away from him. "Would you mind?"

He stood up without speaking and slowly pulled up the little zipper, his fingers strangely gentle for such a big man. She had to move her hair so he didn't snag it near the top.

She shook a little when he finished, and her breathing had gotten ragged.

She was so, so stupid. She wanted Jonathan so much when she'd always known she could never have him.

She took longer than necessary to pick out a pair of heels, mostly so she could hide her face. Then she put on a simple strand of pearls and some earrings.

Jonathan was waiting when she was ready, his shirt more wrinkled than ever.

Automatically, she reached over to smooth out some of the wrinkles before she buttoned his suit jacket.

They went downstairs without speaking, and they'd entered the large, crowded receiving room and gotten their predinner drinks before she remembered she'd forgotten to brush her hair.

~

Jonathan was having trouble keeping his hands off Sarah, so much so that it was becoming ridiculous.

She looked particularly gorgeous this evening with her tousled hair and sleek dress. He knew what she was wearing underneath it. He'd seen the lace bra and the top of what he was sure was a thong as he zipped the dress up for her.

What he'd really wanted to do was take the dress off.

His distracted state was not improved when Sarah drifted away from him while he was making small talk with an old family friend. She went over to talk to Benjamin, who was leaning against a wall on the far side of the room and clearly appearing too bleak and intimidating for many people to greet him.

Sarah showed no reluctance. He'd seen from the window that afternoon when she'd been walking back to the house with Benjamin. They'd seemed very chatty then—as chatty as Benjamin could ever get.

They seemed very chatty now. Sarah was smiling at him warmly as if she liked him.

Jonathan was self-aware enough to know that the brewing tension he felt was jealousy. Possessiveness.

Sarah was supposed to be his fiancée. Even if it was just a ruse, she was still more his than Benjamin's.

His cousin had no right to move into his territory.

Sarah wasn't his territory, however. She wasn't his fiancée. She worked for him, and she had every right to talk to any man she wanted.

But surely she wouldn't blow their whole plan by flirting with his cousin.

She came back over to him before dinner, letting him introduce her as his fiancée to a number of the guests. She was quiet and courteous, and she didn't seem particularly uncomfortable being surrounded by so many strangers.

She would fit in fine here, he realized with an odd twist of his gut. Everyone liked her. His family liked her.

Maybe more than they liked him.

When they went in to dinner, he got another unpleasant revelation. The Damons always placed guests in the old-fashioned way, with couples not seated together. Gordon, probably recognizing that Sarah had made more of a connection to him than anyone else, had placed her next to Benjamin, while Jonathan was all the way down a very long table.

So Jonathan had to watch as they talked all through dinner. Benjamin didn't seem to do much talking, but he looked at her a lot. He even smiled occasionally.

Sarah had called him Ben, as if they were close.

Jonathan was torn between stewing with irrational jealousy and telling himself it was ridiculous all evening. When dinner was over and they went back into the grand parlor for more mingling, he was unsettled, disoriented, and exhausted.

He'd had enough of mingling. Sarah was still talking to Benjamin—they'd been joined by Harrison and Marietta, so at least it wasn't an intimate conversation. She seemed perfectly happy, not even aware of his absence. His uncle was holding court on the other side of the room and hadn't spoken to him all evening.

Jonathan just slipped away.

He could only handle so much socializing before his head exploded, and his confused feelings for Sarah made him want to explode in a different way.

He felt weirdly lonely for no good reason. He never felt that way. He didn't like it.

The only distraction he could come up with was going back to the media room to play Sea and Sky.

It was dead silent on the third floor, so he sat on the floor, took off his jacket, loosened his tie, and cued up the game.

He wasn't sure how long he'd played—maybe an hour or so—when he heard a feminine voice say in the doorway, "There he is. I told you he'd be up here."

He looked over his shoulder and saw Sarah coming into the room with Benjamin behind her.

She smiled at him, although her eyes were unusually sharp as she studied him, as if she were trying to figure out what he was feeling.

He didn't want her to know what he was feeling, so he just offered her the second joystick.

She took it, sitting down next to him as she had the evening before. Her skirt hiked up too high, and he automatically pulled it down for her so Benjamin wouldn't have an inappropriate view of her luscious thighs.

"You could have shared your escape route with us earlier," Benjamin said, coming over to sit on the edge of the couch. His eyes landed on the large monitor. "Damn, I haven't played this game in years."

Jonathan opened a drawer and found a third joystick, giving it to Benjamin in what he thought was a remarkable act of family charity since he'd much rather play with Sarah alone.

The three of them started to play the game without any unnecessary niceties or small talk. All of them were skilled players, and Jonathan was soon absorbed in maintaining his lead. An hour passed quickly until they were interrupted by Harrison and Andrew.

"Is the mingling still going on?" Sarah asked, as the two men came into the room to see what they were doing.

"It's wrapping up," Andrew said. "People are starting to head to their rooms." He looked bored and a little tired, but he perked up when he saw what they were playing. "Wow! That's a blast from the past. Can I play?"

"Sure," Sarah said with a welcoming smile. "Did you want to play too, Harrison?"

Harrison was chuckling under his breath, but he agreed to play—just to be polite, he explained.

"We're not starting over for the two of you," Jonathan said a voice that brooked no arguments. "But we'll

spot you both 50,000 points so you'll have a fighting chance."
He dug up two more joysticks and tossed them over.

Andrew snorted. "You won't have any sort of chance.
I used to be good at this."

Sarah's dress was hiking up again, so Jonathan pulled
it down once more. She slanted him a slightly embarrassed
look and readjusted herself. "Maybe I should go change
clothes," she murmured, looking at him as if she wanted his
opinion.

He was about to say they'd wait for her since it
couldn't be comfortable sitting on the floor in that dress, but
Benjamin said, "I wouldn't. You'd be too far behind by the
time you got back from changing."

She shrugged, and they all focused on the game again.

Jonathan was surprised by how good a time he had
since he thought having his cousins around might be
annoying. But they were all good-natured, and no one was
distracted by conversation. Despite the skill and coordination
of his competitors, Jonathan still held on to the lead.

Sarah was almost as good as he was, and she got more
and more intense as she had to fight to stay in second place.

He hadn't realized she was so competitive before.

Eventually, Laurel and Marietta came in. Laurel
wanted to play, and Harrison offered to give up his spot to
Marietta since the game only allowed six players. Marietta said
she didn't know how to play and she'd be happy to just watch
instead.

"It doesn't seem right that Harrison gets a
cheerleader," Andrew grumbled when Marietta started to

praise and clap for every kill that his brother made, "while my girlfriend is ruthlessly trying to trounce me."

Jonathan found himself laughing with the rest of them—which was an unusual enough circumstance for him notice.

He won the first two games, but they were now on their third.

Harrison and Andrew were hurling insults at each other and occasionally at him. Laurel wasn't as good as the rest of them—since she hadn't had as much practice as a child—but she was watching and evidently taking mental notes since her playing kept getting better and better.

Benjamin wasn't talking, but he was completely absorbed in the game, and he would occasionally smile when someone said something funny or when he made a particularly good move.

Sarah had raised herself up onto her knees, rocking with the intensity with which she maneuvered her joystick. She'd pulled her hair back in a ponytail with a band she'd borrowed from Marietta, and she seemed completely unconscious of her elegant clothes or her undignified position.

Jonathan had never seen anything sexier in his life.

Everyone was getting better as they played, so Jonathan should have been concentrating more closely on the game. But he kept getting distracted by Sarah. By the way her breasts jiggled as she moved the joystick. By the lace tops of her stockings which had slid down and were peeking out beneath her hem. By the idea that all these other men were getting to see her this way.

It was only the distraction that made him miss an obvious kill, only the distraction that allowed Sarah to grab the last starfish before he did.

The room burst into a loud roar of excitement when Sarah won the game, the others clearly elated at the mere fact that someone—anyone—had managed to beat him.

Sarah raised herself higher on her knees, cheering uninhibitedly at her victory. She returned Benjamin's double high five and accepted the loud praise from the others.

Then she turned to Jonathan, beaming, her face spilling over with excitement. "What do you have to say for yourself, loser?"

He tried not to smile in response, but he wasn't entirely successful. He did manage, however, to keep his voice dry as he replied, "I took pity on you and let you win."

The others exclaimed loudly over the injustice of this remark, and Sarah gave him a friendly shove, which caused her to lose her balance and fall against him.

He put his arms around her automatically for support, but it somehow turned into a hug. She had so much warmth and sincerity and passion and brilliance. She was so soft and gorgeous and completely Sarah.

She made everything better.

She made *him* better.

The embrace felt private but wasn't, and no one seemed to think it was strange since they were supposed to be

116

engaged. They were all still talking and laughing, and Sarah was trying to right herself, extricating herself from his arms, when they noticed someone else was in the room.

His uncle stood in the doorway, watching his nephews with an oddly quiet expression on his face.

The laughing and chatting faded when they became aware of his presence.

Cyrus Damon was who he was. He was who he'd always been. And this kind of uproarious, chaotic gathering was nothing like the eminently civil, elegant, formal affairs he favored.

Jonathan felt his stomach drop, although they obviously hadn't been doing anything wrong.

Sarah, however, didn't seem to think anything was strange or uncomfortable. She smiled at his uncle with that same wide, glowing smile and asked, "Did you want to play? You can have my spot if you want. I've already beat all your nephews."

His uncle's expression was surprised, but then it softened into a startlingly kind smile. "No, dear, but thank you. Maybe I'll just watch you beat them again."

CHAPTER SEVEN

Sarah woke up very warm and comfortable again. This morning she immediately knew why.

Once more, she was cuddled up against Jonathan.

It was honestly a little embarrassing—that her sleeping self was so insistent on being close to him. His arm was around her though, holding her body tightly against his side, so at least she wasn't the only one guilty of unconscious snuggling.

She raised her head slightly and was surprised to see in the dim light that his eyes were open.

He'd been staring up at the ceiling, but his eyes shifted to her at her slight motion.

"Hi," she said, smiling a little shyly. After all, it could be a little awkward, cozying up to her boss in bed this way.

"Hi." Jonathan made no move to get up, which surprised her. The previous mornings, he'd rolled out of bed as soon as he was awake. There was a strange look on his face too—thoughtful, almost poignant.

"Are you all right?" she asked, instinctively tightening the arm that was still draped around his middle. When she realized she was hugging his flat, bare belly—that she could feel the thin line of hair that trailed down under his waistband—she drew back her arm immediately.

"Yeah." He didn't pull back his arm or roll away, but he wasn't looking at her anymore.

Since she had nowhere else to put her arm, she laid it back on his abdomen but made sure it was just resting there rather than hugging him. Or stroking him, which was what she really wanted to do.

He didn't say anything else, and she felt another prickle of worry. There was so much going on in his mind that she just didn't know. "Are you sure? You were kind of quiet last night. I mean, after the game."

"We went to bed after the game."

That was true, and he'd never been a big talker, but he'd been unusually withdrawn last night.

"I know." She paused for a moment, struggling over whether she dared to say more. Then, "I thought you had a good time—with the others."

"I did."

She was silent after that since it felt like he had more to say. Intuitively, she knew that if she pressed any further, he would close up and never say it. Her hand flattened on his belly—his flesh warm and firm beneath her palm. It lifted and lowered slightly with his breathing.

After a long stretch of silence, he added, "I never expected to have a good time with them."

The words were vague, almost diffident, but she understood them immediately. He'd never felt a part of a family that way. The idea made her incredibly sad. "I think your uncle was surprised too. But he seemed to... he seemed to enjoy it. I think."

"Yeah. It was…"

"It was what?" She was almost holding her breath, wondering what he would say.

"It was strange. I've always thought I would never be able to do enough to earn his respect or… appreciation, but last night… when I wasn't even trying…"

She swallowed hard, wanting to say so much but terrified of saying anything—of stepping over some line. She finally murmured, "Maybe it's not about earning it."

He didn't reply, but he didn't seem to resent what she'd said.

They lay together in silence for a few more minutes, until Sarah realized she was caressing his belly after all. Her hand was under the sheet, but she glanced down at it anyway.

When she did, she saw something else.

He was hard.

The knowledge did something dangerous in her chest and between her legs. She'd never really thought she was the kind of woman who would turn on a man like Jonathan. Sure, if he was half-asleep in a dark room, but not just lying together in the morning light.

But maybe… maybe…

She darted a glance up to his face, with a jittery hope that she'd see heat, desire, or at least some sort of physical interest.

Instead, he just gave a half shrug, obviously realizing what she'd noticed. "It's morning."

Comprehension dropped on her like a brick. His hard-on wasn't about her after all—just a normal morning erection.

"Yeah," she said, trying for a casual smile. "Must be very inconvenient for you."

He did roll away then and climbed out of bed. As he walked to the bathroom, she took an automatic assessment of the smoothly rippling muscles of his shoulders and back, his firm butt under his shorts, and his strong, hairy legs. He looked masculine, virile, incredibly domestic.

She wanted him desperately—and not just physically—but he didn't want her at all.

~

At breakfast that morning, Sarah was still worried about Jonathan. It seemed like something was brewing inside him that he couldn't acknowledge, much less admit aloud.

Thinking it might help if he could get away from the estate for a while and feel more himself again, she suggested at breakfast that she wouldn't mind doing a little sightseeing, since this was the last day before the wedding festivities started in earnest.

She wanted to see Bath since she'd always been a big Jane Austen fan. She also wanted to see Stonehenge since it wasn't far from Bath.

Jonathan agreed to take her, and she was pleased with the success of her plan—especially since she caught a faint glimpse of relief in his eyes as if he liked the idea.

Then Ben, who'd been reading a newspaper and drinking coffee across the table, asked, "Were you hoping for it to be romantic, or are others allowed to tag along?"

Sarah was surprised by the request, but she wasn't upset or disappointed. It definitely wasn't a romantic outing, and having someone else there would help her to remember that lest she get carried away again. Besides, Ben was obviously desperate to escape from the manor for a while, and she couldn't help but take pity on him.

She liked him more than she'd expected to on first meeting. He was certainly bitter and isolated, but he was also clever, observant, and surprisingly funny. So she smiled at him brightly and said she'd be happy for him to join them if Jonathan didn't mind.

She looked over at Jonathan. "Is that all right, honey? Can Ben come?" She wasn't quite sure why she added the endearment, but she suspected they weren't doing a very good job of acting like a couple, and it seemed like a "honey" moment.

He blinked at her. "Sure."

He didn't say anything else, but that wasn't unusual for Jonathan. So Sarah assumed they were all satisfied with the arrangement.

~

Sarah was glad Ben had come along after all since Jonathan was very bad company that day.

She had no idea what was wrong with him. He wasn't his normal, matter-of-fact self. He was curt, grumpy, and occasionally even rude—and it seemed to get worse as the morning progressed.

Bath was only a half hour from the manor, so they got there early. They went through the Roman baths and the Jane Austen museum. Then they just wandered the quaint streets, admiring the architecture and stopping for coffee in a charming tearoom.

Sarah would have had a very good time if Jonathan hadn't been acting like an ass.

At least Ben was better company.

He certainly wasn't charming or talkative, but Sarah was good with laconic men. After all, she'd spent three years working with Jonathan. She soon grew to realize that Ben wasn't anything like Jonathan. He wasn't reserved by nature the way Jonathan was. If he hadn't been so cynical and scarred, he probably would have been as charming and charismatic as Andrew. When she managed to get him talking about books or history, he was really quite interesting and compelling.

He had no interest in Jane Austen, but then neither did Jonathan. They both traipsed through the sites with her though, Ben mocking her enthusiasm and Jonathan saying nothing at all.

They decided to have lunch before they headed over to Stonehenge. When Ben got up to go to the bathroom, Sarah had had enough.

"What the hell is wrong with you?" she gritted out, keeping her voice low so the nearby tables couldn't hear.

Jonathan had been staring down at his empty plate, but he looked over at her now with raised eyebrows. "Nothing's wrong."

"That's obviously a lie. You've been an asshole all morning."

"I haven't said anything rude or inappropriate."

She gave a huff of indignation. "You haven't said anything *at all*, and you've flat out ignored half what Ben has said. He's really trying."

Something grew cold and still in Jonathan's eyes— something she couldn't begin to understand. "Trying to do what?"

Her mouth dropped open in astonishment and incomprehension. "Trying to be nice. He's your cousin, and you barely ever see him. The least you could do is meet him halfway. Jonathan, he's trying to be nice."

"Is that what you think?"

The words were so uncharacteristically clipped that she suddenly understood something. "Are you angry with *me*?" she asked.

He just looked at her. Didn't say anything. And she knew, just from the expression in his eyes and the tension on his face, that there was something major going on inside him that he hadn't even begun to express.

She wanted to shake it out of him. She was suddenly so angry she could have slapped him. "Damn it, Jonathan," she hissed. "You're the most frustrating man in the world. If you're upset about something, you need to say it. I have no idea what I've done, so it's never going to get better if you don't tell me."

She stared at him, flushed and panting. He just looked back at her. His breathing had picked up too, and his hand had fisted on his lap, but he gave no other sign of what was bothering him.

"Why the hell can't you say it?" she demanded. "If you're mad at me, I need to know why."

For just a moment, she thought he was going to tell her—it was like something was coiled inside him, ready to spring free.

But then he let out a breath and looked away. "I'm not mad at you, Sarah. You haven't done anything wrong."

She knew she hadn't done anything wrong, but she still wanted to know what had upset him. Gazing at his handsome and now passive face for several seconds, she realized she wasn't going to know.

It was just midday, but he needed to shave again. She could see the dark bristles on his strong jaw. She wanted to stroke them, to feel them beneath her hand.

She wanted to hit him and take care of him both. It was a very disorienting feeling.

"Jonathan?" she asked thickly.

He just shook his head.

She gave up and finished off the sparkling water in her glass. And then she realized that he was still her boss, and she'd spoken to him in a way that might be considered inappropriate.

"Sorry I yelled at you," she said sheepishly. She hadn't really raised her voice, but she'd definitely spoken harshly, more harshly than she ever had before. She didn't think he would fire her for something like that, but it would better if their relationship returned to somewhat professional grounds.

"Don't be sorry," he murmured, heaving himself up to his feet as if it were hard to make himself move. "I deserved it. I'm going to get more coffee."

He went back inside the tearoom just as Ben was coming out. He didn't greet his cousin.

When he returned to the table, Ben slouched down in his chair and gave her a half smile.

"Sorry," she said, nodding toward where Jonathan had walked into the building. "He's not himself today. He's not a big talker, but he's usually polite. I don't know what's gotten into him."

"Don't you?" Ben asked, looking amused.

Sarah's eyes widened. "What do you mean?"

He didn't answer, and once more Sarah had the almost irresistible impulse to shake an answer out of a close-mouthed asshole.

Instead of answering, Ben looked from the spot in the air he'd been staring at and met her eyes without warning. "You're not really engaged to him, are you?"

She froze. "What?"

"I've been trying to figure you two out, and there's no way you're really engaged."

"Yes, we are," she argued lamely.

"Is it some sort of plot to trick Lord Uncle into leaving him alone? If so, I heartily approve."

Sarah didn't reply, just sat tensely, trapped and terrified. If she'd somehow given them away, if Jonathan would lose everything because of it, then she'd never forgive herself.

"I'm not going to tell," Ben added. "Your secret is safe with me."

She studied him closely, desperately, and concluded he was telling the truth. She relaxed a little. She hadn't admitted anything, after all, and Ben had no love or obligation toward his uncle that would compel him to share his suspicions.

He glanced over toward the tearoom, where Jonathan was emerging with a full cup of coffee. Then, with an almost naughty glint in his eye, Ben reached over and picked up her hand.

He looked down at her finger. "It's a really nice ring," he drawled, "For a fake engagement, I mean. How long did he take picking it out for you?"

~

Jonathan had only been gone for a few minutes, but when he returned Benjamin was holding Sarah's hand.

She withdrew it almost immediately, but she was prettily flushed and flustered. A wave of jealousy slammed into him, so intense it almost consumed him.

Sarah was his.

At least, that was how it felt.

He'd never been a violent man, but the thought of her with Ben made him want to smash something. Preferably, his cousin's face.

He stopped walking until he could control the feeling. He had no claim on Sarah except as an employer. It wasn't fair and it wasn't reasonable to expect her to act like they were in a relationship.

He'd spent his life trying not to be irrational, to work hard and accomplish something worthwhile with his intellect and his persistence. He wasn't going to throw it all away now for something so ephemeral.

If Sarah wanted to be with Ben, if she wanted Ben's company over Jonathan's, then he would have to live with it and he would have no grounds for complaining.

Sarah wasn't his.

When he felt like he had himself back under control, he walked over to their table. "Ready to go?" he asked, pleased that his voice sounded natural.

Ben was smiling smugly, as if he knew something Jonathan didn't. Maybe he knew he'd taken Sarah away from him.

"Yes, we're ready," Sarah said, standing up. She still seemed flustered, and she stumbled a little as she took a step away from the table.

Jonathan reached out instinctively to help, and she grabbed onto his shirt to stabilize herself. His arm tightened around her, pressing her soft body against him.

She gazed up at him with flushed cheeks and heavy eyelids, her lips so full and kissable he almost couldn't resist.

"Sorry," she said, lowering her eyes and pulling away. "Just clumsy today, I guess."

For some reason, Benjamin laughed.

~

The afternoon and evening seemed endless to Jonathan. They visited Stonehenge, which didn't take long since after they walked around the roped off path and took some pictures, there wasn't much else to do. Then they drove back, and Sarah got ready for Marietta's wedding shower.

Since Jonathan had a free afternoon, he tried to work on e-mail. But he hated doing e-mail and he couldn't seem to focus, so he gave up and worked out instead. He ran hard on the treadmill, but it did little to ease the tension in his mind.

That evening, they had the bachelor and bachelorette parties.

There wasn't a stripper at the bachelor party since Cyrus Damon was paying for it and Harrison wasn't really that kind of man anyway. They went to a local pub and drank beers, and Harrison's friends and Andrew told jokes and tried to embarrass Harrison with stories from his past.

Jonathan didn't have a bad time. He might have even enjoyed it if Benjamin hadn't been there giving him knowing, amused looks.

It was late when they got home, and Jonathan was surprised to discover that Sarah hadn't returned yet. He didn't know what the women had done, but he'd (perhaps ignorantly) expected them to be done earlier than the men.

Jonathan took a shower and was reading in bed when there was a knock on the bedroom door.

He was surprised to see that Gordon had walked up with Sarah, carrying her purse and sweater. Then he realized why the butler had done so.

Sarah had clearly had a little too much to drink.

Fortunately, Jonathan had pulled on a T-shirt when the knock on the door came. He wouldn't want to talk to Gordon in just his underwear.

Sarah giggled when he opened the door. "There he is. My fiancé." She drawled out the last word unnaturally long.

Jonathan met Gordon's eyes.

"My apologies for disturbing you, sir, but I thought I should make sure she got to her room all right."

"I only got lost once," she declared, clearly offended by some imagined slight to her sense of direction. She grabbed fistfuls of Jonathan's T-shirt and slumped against him. "I had a really good time at the bachelorette party."

"I can see that," he said. He glanced over her head at Gordon. "What did they do?"

"They went to a club, sir."

"Hey," Sarah objected, glaring at Gordon. "I was going to tell him. We danced a lot."

She started to show him, swinging her hips and waving her arms. "I was very sexy."

"I'm sure you were," he murmured, putting an arm around her waist so she wouldn't dance her way down the hall. "Thanks, Gordon."

"Do you need anything, sir? Some more water, perhaps?" It seemed impossible that Gordon wasn't a little amused by Sarah's antics, but there wasn't a trace of laughter in his placid blue eyes as he handed Jonathan her purse and sweater.

"We still have a couple of bottles here. Thank you."

"Make out with me, Jonathan," Sarah mumbled, as he tried to pull her into the room. She was pressed up against him, her lush body rubbing against his in a way that was very distracting. "I want you to make out with me."

"Maybe later." He managed to guide her into the room, gently pushing her toward the bed. "You should lie down now. How much did you have to drink?"

"A couple of glasses of wine," she huffed, still rubbing up against him.

When she'd left earlier that evening, she'd been wearing a little cashmere cardigan over her dress, and he was alarmed at how much the dress actually revealed.

It was strapless and not very long, and it had discreet sparkles in the dark green fabric. She looked absolutely delectable, but he hated the idea of who knew how many other men seeing her this way.

The neckline kept slipping down as she rubbed against him, and the sight of her lush cleavage and the insistent rubbing had a predictable effect on his body.

Even in her muddled state, she noticed it almost immediately and started rubbing up more strategically against his groin.

He almost groaned at the sensations but managed to summon enough willpower to gently push her away. "Let's not do that right now."

"I *want* to do that."

"I don't think you really do." He maneuvered her onto the edge of the bed and knelt down to take off her shoes.

She stretched her foot out until it was pushing into his shoulder, showing him much too much very sexy leg. "Do you like my stockings?"

He did like them. A lot. But he couldn't let him himself admire them at the moment. Looking down at the shoe in his hand, he said, "They're very nice. Now, why don't you get in bed?"

"Jon-athan,"

His body tightened at the throaty word. It sounded exactly the way she'd said his name during sex.

"Jonathan," she said again, louder and more insistent.

Since her voice didn't sound like sex, he looked up to meet her eyes.

"I have something to tell you." She leaned over, a sweet but blurry expression on her face.

"I'm listening."

"It's a secret," she whispered, her eyes darting around as if someone might be listening. She reached out, grabbed the shoulder of his shirt, and pulled him closer.

Irrational or not, it felt like she was going to say something significant, something he would want to hear. Maybe it was less than ethical to listen to intimate revelations while she was intoxicated—and he knew enough to know they couldn't always be trusted—but he tensed up anyway, waiting.

"Jon-athan," she murmured throatily into his ear. "I'm not wearing any underwear."

He let out a huff of dry amusement and also lust at the image the words conjured up. But he steeled his will and asked, "Do you need to go to the bathroom?"

"Yeah. You're a very smart man, you know."

He helped her to her feet and then to the bathroom, but there he left her to her own devices since he was quite sure she wouldn't appreciate his watching her pee.

After he heard the toilet flush, the water ran for a long time in the sink, so long he finally tapped on the door. "Sarah? Everything all right?"

He pushed the door open and found her with her hands stuck under the running faucet, staring at herself fixedly in the mirror. He went over to turn the water off, dried her hands with a towel, and then put his palm on her back to urge her back toward the bed.

She sat on the edge of the bed again where he put her and didn't move. But she raised her hands when he brought an oversized T-shirt over and helped her put it on. Fortunately, her dress was strapless, so he could just pull it off under the shirt without any inappropriate leering.

She was still sitting on the edge of the bed when he handed her a bottle of water. She made a face. "I don't want water." She seemed to have passed the silly stage of her intoxication and moved into the pitiful stage.

"You will later," he said, placing it on the nightstand beside her bed. "Why don't you lie down now?"

She scooted under the covers obediently. He went to the bathroom, turned out the lights, and got into bed beside her.

She immediately edged over and burrowed into his side. Since there was nothing else to do with his arm, he put it around her.

"I had fun tonight," she said to the dark room.

"I'm glad."

"I danced."

"That's what you said earlier."

"A lot of men came on to me."

He swallowed. "I'm not surprised."

She was silent for a long time, and he thought she'd gone to sleep. But then she said, her voice softer, almost broken, "I wish you liked me."

"I do like you." He said it instinctively because he didn't like the catch in her voice, and it didn't feel dangerous because she was so far out of it.

"I wish you thought I was pretty."

"I do think you're pretty." He never would have said such a thing at any other time, but she felt small and needy, huddled up against him.

"You don't really."

Yes, she was tipsy. Yes, she never would have said such a thing had she been in her normal state. But he somehow knew she believed it—she actually believed he didn't think she was pretty.

The knowledge roused in him such an astonished indignation that he burst out, "Don't be ridiculous, Sarah. You're the most beautiful woman I know."

The grumpy words hung in the air. She didn't reply immediately, just nestled against him some more.

She probably wouldn't even remember them when she woke up tomorrow morning.

"Oh," she whispered at last. "Thank you. I'm glad."

The words sounded more lucid than anything else she'd said that evening, so Jonathan bent his head to peer at her in the dark, wondering if she was sober again.

But she'd just fallen asleep.

Jonathan didn't sleep, not for a really long time. He lay awake in bed, hour after hour, holding her in his arms.

CHAPTER EIGHT

Sarah woke up with a dull headache and a disgusting taste in her mouth.

She rolled over, blinking vaguely at the empty other side of the bed, her fuzzy mind noting that it was rumpled as if someone had slept there.

She rolled over to the other side and saw a bottle of water on the nightstand, like a boon from the gods. She grabbed at it and gulped down several mouthfuls, choking slightly since she hadn't sat all the way up.

She made herself sit up then, even though her head pounded even more. She breathed and kept drinking the water until her mind cleared enough to realize where she was and how she'd gotten into this state.

She'd made a fool of herself last night.

She almost never drank. She'd never had much of a social life in high school or college—certainly not the kind that did a lot of partying. So the most she ever drank was a glass or two of wine at dinner on those few occasions she went out.

She didn't know why she'd drunk so much last night—except she'd been feeling pretty and was determined not to be depressed over Jonathan's lack of interest in her.

She closed her eyes, trying to recall if she'd done anything too humiliating, anything she couldn't take back.

The water was lukewarm from sitting beside her bed all night, which wasn't particularly pleasant, but at least it was wet. It was almost eight. Jonathan had probably gotten up more than an hour ago and gone down to breakfast.

Quite stupidly, she missed him.

As if her thoughts had summoned him, he walked into the room, dressed in wrinkled khakis and a black golf shirt and carrying a bottle of water.

"This one's cold," he said, handing it to her as if nothing at all were strange about her condition.

She took it gratefully and gulped down a few more swallows.

"How do you feel?" he asked. He was rooting through a drawer as if he were searching for something, but she could see him giving her a sidelong look of scrutiny.

"Like a fool," she admitted croakily.

"Don't. You just had a little too much to drink. Happens to everyone."

"It's never happened to me before."

"You've really never been drunk?"

She shook her head and drank more water, this time mostly as a distraction. "I had very vanilla teenage years."

His mouth quirked up in a half smile. "Somehow, that doesn't surprise me." His tone was warm, almost fond, but Sarah was hurt by the words just the same.

Evidently, he thought she was so boring she couldn't even misbehave.

"What's wrong?" he asked, his eyebrows drawing together. He was studying her again and must have noticed her reaction.

"Nothing. Just a headache."

"You want some aspirin?"

"Not yet. Not sure my stomach could take it."

"Do you remember anything from last night?" The words were strangely diffident, as if he were trying for them to not sound significant.

She was suddenly terrified, her queasy stomach tightening into a hard knot. Had she done something to Jonathan, said something she shouldn't have said? Was that why he looked so wary?

"I remember some," she said slowly, trying to sort out the tangle of images in her mind. "We were dancing at the club. I was having fun, I think."

She *had* been having fun. She'd never been much of a dancer, but after a couple of drinks she'd lost her inhibitions. She'd felt wild and sexy, and she'd been thrilled by all the male attention she'd received.

It was an entirely new experience for her—that she might be the kind of woman that strangers were attracted to.

"I don't think I did anything too bad or stupid," she muttered, closing her eyes again as she thought. "I didn't make out with a stranger or anything."

"That's good." He looked more relaxed, and he was half smiling again. "No harm done then."

Sarah was starting to feel a little better too when she was hit by a crystal-clear memory. "Oh, God," she groaned. "Did I... did I try to make out with *you?*"

She had. She remembered it now. She'd been babbling like an idiot and rubbing herself up against him like a horny tramp. "Oh, God," she moaned again.

"Don't worry about it." He sounded matter-of-fact, unconcerned, but he was still rooting around in that drawer.

It wasn't that big a drawer. What the hell was he trying to find?

"I'm so sorry," she mumbled, covering her hot face with her hands. "I can't believe I did that."

"Don't worry about it," he repeated, looking over at her at last. "I know enough not to take anything seriously that happens after that many drinks."

"But I..." He was her boss, and not only had she behaved like a fool but she'd also talked to and touched him quite inappropriately. She had a horrific image of rubbing her leg against him, asking if he liked her stockings.

She looked down at herself. She was still wearing her stockings. And an oversized T-shirt that must belong to him.

She pushed her stockings down her legs like they were poisoned, yanking them off with little regard for their delicacy or expense.

"Seriously, Sarah," Jonathan said, coming over to stand beside the bed and gently pulling her up to her feet by one arm. "Don't be embarrassed. It's nothing I'm ever going to think about or hold against you. I've done silly things before too."

She gazed up at him, her belly twisting again, but this time with a deep, fond emotion. His dark eyes were unusually intense, but so kind they made her want to melt. "I don't think you've done silly things," she murmured stupidly.

"Believe me. I have." He let go of her and went back to the mysterious drawer of hidden treasures he couldn't seem to get his hands on.

She watched him in silence for a minute. His thick, gentle voice sounded familiar, and she was starting to remember why.

He'd been speaking to her in that tone last night, all through her ridiculous antics. And he'd said things. She could remember them now.

He'd said he liked her. That she was pretty. That she was the most beautiful woman he knew.

And she suddenly realized why he was pretending to look for something in the drawer. He was self-conscious, uncomfortable, needed a distraction.

Jonathan Damon wasn't a man who gave empty compliments. He was never charming, and he didn't say things just to please or appease someone else.

He never said things he didn't mean.

She was suddenly slammed with a blinding hope.

He'd been hard last night, aroused. By her. She remembered that now too. And he'd been so incredibly sweet, in a characteristically Jonathan way.

Maybe she'd been wrong about him. Maybe she'd been wrong about everything.

~

Jonathan left the room before Sarah could fully process the realization. Gordon came up shortly afterward with breakfast on a tray and some aspirin, which he said Jonathan had suggested.

Sarah ate what she could, and she was starting to feel better after she got dressed.

She wasn't sure whether it was the shower, the aspirin, or the chaos of jittery excitement that had so thoroughly changed her condition.

There was lunch and croquet on the lawn that day, and the hours passed in a fuzzy haze. She smiled, chatted with strangers, and stood with Jonathan the whole time, fielding awkward questions like when they were going to tie the knot and whether they wanted children as smoothly and vaguely as she could.

Maybe it was her imagination, but Jonathan seemed different too. Less standoffish. More solicitous. He kept his hand on the small of her back when they were talking to other guests, and she loved how it felt there.

She tried to tell herself to be reasonable, that just because he thought she was pretty—the most beautiful woman he knew—didn't mean he had or could have serious feelings about her.

He was still her boss, after all, and that would always make things tricky.

Despite her mental lecturing, she was feeling increasingly bouncy anyway.

After croquet, she had a few free hours before the rehearsal dinner. Jonathan was pulled into some sort of discussion with his uncle, so she grabbed her e-reader and headed to the secret garden.

She tried to read but couldn't focus. She fiddled with her ring and kept thinking about Jonathan. What he might say, what she might say, how she could possibly find out whether there was any hope of a relationship with him. If there was any way to work it out with her job.

It made her nervous since she didn't want to be crushed. But she couldn't help but put together hints and pieces in her mind and come up with the conclusion that she must be more to him than just an assistant.

She wanted to be so much more.

~

Jonathan couldn't find Sarah, and it was starting to annoy him.

He'd showered and dressed in a dark suit for the rehearsal dinner, and it was nearly time for them to go down to dinner.

She wasn't in the room. According to Gordon, she wasn't in the house.

He tried to be reasonable and tell himself she'd just lost track of time. But she was never late. She was always responsible.

Something had happened or something had seriously distracted her.

He paced the bedroom, looking out the window onto the lawn and then looking out into the hallway in sequence.

He couldn't imagine she would have gotten hurt. She wouldn't have driven anywhere or done anything physical— not in the couple of hours between wedding events.

He'd thought she would have just taken a nap since she hadn't gotten much sleep the night before.

He'd seen her with Benjamin after the croquet was breaking up. Surely she wouldn't have gone off with him.

She'd seemed different today, more responsive. There'd been an almost intimate look in her eyes.

As he'd been talking to family friends and family members on the lawn of his uncle's estate, it had felt like she was really his fiancée.

It had felt like she was *his*.

Which was why he reacted so strongly to the fact that she might have gone off with Benjamin.

He went downstairs and asked Gordon again if he'd seen her.

Gordon hadn't. He would get some of the staff to search the grounds for her if he liked.

Jonathan didn't want to overreact, so he said they could wait a little while longer.

He went out onto the back patio to look out on the gardens and was surprised to see Benjamin lounging in a chair and reading from an e-reader.

Benjamin still had the beard and untrimmed hair, but he'd made some sort of effort for the occasion, wearing black trousers and a black dress shirt.

"What's up?" he asked, evidently noticing Jonathan's expression.

"Nothing. Just looking for Sarah."

"I think she was going to read in the garden earlier. You might check out the walled garden in the east corner near the woods. That's where she was reading yesterday. You better hurry though. Lord Uncle won't appreciate a late arrival to dinner."

Jonathan nodded and headed in that direction, telling himself it was ridiculous to be annoyed that Benjamin knew more about Sarah's doings than he did. Instead, he should just be relieved that she hadn't been with him.

It took him a few minutes to actually find the walled garden and then another few minutes to find the door. At least it wasn't locked.

He found Sarah immediately. She was stretched out on the hammock, sound asleep.

He smiled as he leaned over her. She looked absolutely scrumptious, her red hair spilled out around her face and her fair skin flushed from sleep. Her body was relaxed, one hand resting on her stomach.

He leaned down and gently touched her shoulder. "Sarah."

She mumbled and tried to roll away.

"Sarah," he said again, louder. He shook her very gently.

She came awake suddenly, her eyes popping open and her slow breathing hitching into a gasp.

He felt strangely tender, strangely protective—as if this lush, generous woman was his to take care of.

Her blue eyes focused on his face, and she smiled up at him sleepily.

He smiled back.

"What happened?" she asked, her voice breaking on the second word.

"You fell asleep."

She blinked at him. "Why are you all dressed up?"

"It's time for dinner."

"Oh." She looked away from him, clearly processing this piece of knowledge. Then, "Oh. Oh no! I fell asleep. What time is it?"

"It's seven-thirty."

"I'm late!" She grabbed his arm and used it to haul herself to her feet. "I'm not even dressed. I'm so sorry."

"Don't worry about it," he said, still smiling rather goofily.

"Your uncle will be upset. You go on to dinner, and I'll get dressed really quick."

They started walking quickly, pausing only to lock the garden door and put the key behind the stone.

"I'm not going to go to dinner without you. It's not a big deal."

"It *is* a big deal," she insisted, "Your uncle takes these things seriously. And this is an important dinner. Why didn't you wake me up earlier?"

She sounded really upset and was starting to get out of breath since she was practically running down the garden path toward the house.

"I didn't know where you were," he explained, lengthening his stride to keep up with her.

"I know. It's not your fault. I'm so sorry."

"You don't have to be sorr—" He cut off the word since she obviously wasn't listening, so focused was she on getting back to the house as quickly as possible.

It took a few minutes to get to the house and then another minute or two to sprint up flights of stairs to their room.

Then she yanked her shirt and skirt off and dropped them on the floor as she hurried toward the closet.

Jonathan wanted to be a gentleman but couldn't help but stare at her shapely back, bottom, and legs, covered only in a skimpy lace bra and panties.

She grabbed an evening gown of bronze silk and pulled it over her head, letting the slinky fabric slide over her curves. "Can you zip?" she asked, hurrying over to the case on the dresser where she kept her jewelry.

He walked over as she pulled out a pair of antique-looking earrings and fumbled to put them in her ears.

He reached down toward the zipper of the dress that was hanging open. Her smooth back was completely exposed, except for the lace strip of her bra.

He stared down at the graceful contour leading down toward her waist and rounded hips. Her hair was wildly tousled, swaying over her shoulders as she fiddled with her earrings.

Jonathan experienced a surge of yearning so powerful he could barely process it.

He wanted this woman—he *wanted* her—so deeply he momentarily couldn't breathe.

It wasn't just physical. He wanted her in every way.

He wanted her to be his.

"Jonathan, zip," she urged impatiently, looking at him over her shoulder.

He zipped her dress up and dropped his hands.

She turned around, working on the clasp on her necklace that matched the earrings. "Do I look okay?" she asked anxiously.

His eyes devoured her. The slinky bronze dress flattered her figure and brought out the paleness of her skin, the vividness of her hair. Her skin was a little dewy from her haste, and her hair was sexily mussed.

"You look…" She was the most beautiful thing he'd ever seen. He swallowed. "Fine."

"Are you sure? Do I stink?"

She smelled like Sarah and sunshine and grass, and it roused something primitive in his body, in his heart. "You smell fine."

Her face twisted in distress. "I wanted to look all gorgeous tonight, but we don't have time. Let's go."

"Sarah," he said, stopping her with a hand on her arm. "Wait."

He wanted to tell her she did look gorgeous, that he'd never wanted anyone more.

She turned around and gazed up at him, her expression changing from impatience to something startlingly soft.

His chest clamped down around his voice. "You need to put on some shoes."

~

Cyrus Damon shot Jonathan a cool glance as he and Sarah slipped into the huge ornate ballroom, which was set up for a formal dinner party.

They were twenty minutes late, and his uncle wasn't likely to let that go unnoticed.

Fortunately, they were sitting on the very end of the main table, so they didn't make a huge scene taking their seats.

The guests were still on the salad course, and they hadn't missed any of the toasts, so Jonathan was satisfied that their lateness wasn't a big deal.

Sarah stirred her salad in her plate and slanted him an anxious look. "I'm so sorry."

"Stop it, Sarah," he said under his breath. "You have nothing to be sorry about. It's not a big deal."

"I'm supposed to be helping with your uncle, not getting him mad at you."

"He likes you. He won't be that annoyed." When she still looked worried, he took her face in one hand. Murmured, "I mean it, Sarah. It's not your job to please my uncle."

Her eyes were wide and soft. "It's not? I thought that's why I was here."

It was. That was the whole point of his ruse. No wonder she was so flustered. She wouldn't know he didn't care about the ruse anymore. That he wanted it to be real.

But had no idea how to make it so.

"Don't worry about it," he said thickly, putting his hand down before he did something stupid like pull her into a kiss.

"Okay." She looked down at her plate, then back up to him. She smiled and reached over toward him.

For a moment, he thought she was going to caress his face, but her fingers glided over his hair instead. "You should have combed your hair," she said with a teasing smile.

"Is it bad?" He wasn't surprised, what with the frustrating search for her, the rush back to the house, and the rampant lust.

She smoothed it down, her lips quivering. "Not too bad."

He was pretty sure she was lying, but he didn't give a damn about his hair.

When Sarah started on her salad again, looking more relaxed, he glanced over at his uncle, who was watching him thoughtfully.

Jonathan looked away, and his eyes landed on Andrew. Andrew was watching him too, for some reason, and was wearing an expression of barely concealed hilarity.

Jonathan wasn't always up on social nuances, but he knew instinctively what had amused his cousin.

He and Sarah had arrived late to dinner, and they were both tousled and flushed. Andrew, naturally, would assume they were doing something other than rushing from the garden.

If only that were the case.

CHAPTER NINE

Sarah felt absolutely beautiful.

It was a rare enough feeling for her to be rather overwhelmed by it. She kept wanting to giggle or hug herself.

She didn't, of course. She was walking into the four-hundred-year-old chapel on Damon manor beside Jonathan in front of the eyes of two hundred guests, so she kept a composed smile on her face.

Inside, she was giddy though.

She wore an elegant gown of slate blue silk since the wedding was black tie. It had vintage-looking lace straps and cinched in a thick band just under her breasts. She wore it with a fine-webbed silk cardigan since she didn't want to flash too much skin at an old-fashioned wedding.

Jonathan had stared at her speechlessly when she'd come out of the bathroom fully dressed, but she'd learned to read him better during the past week, and she was sure it was admiration in his eyes.

When she walked down the center aisle of the chapel with Jonathan toward the family pews in the front, she was conscious that other guests were watching her. But she felt pretty, so it was an excited kind of self-consciousness rather than the old familiar kind that made her want to sink into the floor.

Sarah had always known she was smart. And she'd always known she was competent and successful at the things she tried her hand to. She knew some men had liked her, even wanted to have sex with her. But she'd always assumed they were settling for her looks because they liked other things about her.

Most women, she assumed, became aware of their power to attract men sometime in their teens. For Sarah, it was only happening now.

Which might have been why she, at the moment, felt like a silly adolescent girl on her way to the prom.

Jonathan put his hand on the small of her back to guide her to the pew the usher was gesturing them into. He looked startlingly handsome in his traditional tux—more like a sexy secret agent from a movie than the rumpled, brilliant man she knew.

She slid in the pew to sit beside Ben, who was actually wearing a tuxedo too. The contrast between the sophisticated suit and his unruly beard was odd but still attractive.

She grinned at him and leaned over to whisper that he looked good and he should wear a tux more often.

Jonathan had been quiet since they'd gotten dressed for the wedding. Even quieter than usual for him. He was giving her an oddly cool look now, like he was displeased about something. But he put his arm on the back of the pew behind her shoulders when they sat down, and she loved the way it felt, like he was claiming her, protecting her.

The chapel was decorated beautifully in white roses, pink tulips, and purple orchids. There were candles at all the stained-glass windows and more at the front around the altar.

When Harrison took his place at the front next to Andrew—both looking like movie stars in their tuxes—Sarah felt a brief surge of envy. Harrison was one of the most controlled, confident men she'd ever encountered. Yet he looked antsy, almost anxious, standing in the front. Not like he was scared or reluctant to take this big step, but like he was desperately anxious for it to happen.

He loved Marietta that much.

Sarah had never really believed a man could ever love and want her like that, but now the recognition ached.

She didn't just want any faceless man to love her like that—the way she had in so many of her youthful daydreams. She wanted *Jonathan* to. And not as a dream hero, but as a flesh-and-blood man.

Laurel was Marietta's only attendant, and she walked down the aisle first. Sarah saw Andrew wink at her, and Laurel give him a discreet, disapproving shake of her head, all the while hiding a smile.

Then the music swelled and everyone stood up. Sarah couldn't see much past Jonathan's broad shoulder and the people behind them, but she knew Marietta had started down the aisle.

She glanced back toward Harrison, whom she could see better. He was gazing at Marietta, and Sarah had to turn away from what she saw on his face.

Her chest hurt for no good reason. No good reason at all.

Marietta had now gotten far enough up the aisle for Sarah to see her. She was escorted by an older man. Vern Edwards, Marietta's grandfather. Sarah had met him last night. He was very clearly almost in tears now.

Marietta's dress had probably cost a fortune, but it was simply cut with thick straps, a square neckline, and a fitted bodice that flared out into a princess skirt. It wasn't what Sarah would have chosen for a wedding dress, but it was innocent and delicately pretty—much like Marietta herself.

Marietta had told Sarah a couple of nights ago at her bachelorette party that Harrison was the only man she'd ever had sex with.

Sarah's throat was hurting now, and her hands were trembling. She had no idea why.

They'd reached the minister at the front of the chapel, and Edwards kissed Marietta's cheek and went to sit down.

Harrison and Marietta stood side by side. He didn't look at anyone but her.

It was a beautiful wedding—with every detail pitch perfect. Harrison and Marietta obviously loved each other deeply. But there wasn't anything unusual about the wedding, and Sarah didn't even know the couple very well. She'd been to dozens of weddings before and had never felt this way.

But for no good reason, her eyes burned with tears.

She twisted her hands together in her lap nervously, trying to focus on anything but her ridiculous emotional response. She shifted in her seat.

155

The minister was talking now, and then Cyrus Damon got up to read a passage from the book of Isaiah about how the sin and death and tears of the world would all be remade in love and new life.

And Sarah couldn't sit still, afraid at any moment she was going to break down and cry.

She wasn't a woman who did that. She never cried at weddings. She didn't cry much at all. None of this made any sense.

Without even looking at her, Jonathan reached over and covered her twisting hands on her lap with one of his big, warm ones, maybe to keep her still or maybe to comfort her. She didn't know. It stilled her fidgeting immediately.

It also made her lose it.

Her shoulders shook, and the tears she'd been trying to keep in her eyes spilled out to stream down her face. She ducked her head, wishing she'd worn her hair loose so it could hide her face. But it was pulled back in an elegant chignon at the nape of her neck and offered no protection.

When she didn't pull it together in a few moments, Ben nudged her with his elbow, giving her a look that was obviously a question about whether she was all right.

She smiled and made a helpless gesture, trying to signal that she had no idea what was wrong but it was no big deal.

Jonathan had let go of her hands when she'd gestured to Ben, and now he put his arm around her shoulder. He still hadn't looked at her. She had no idea what he was thinking.

Maybe he would think it was just that time of the month. Maybe he would think she was someone who always cried at weddings. Maybe he would think she was one of those pitiful women who cried because she wanted this for herself so much and could never have it.

She wouldn't have been able to explain it anyway since she had no idea why she was crying.

Marietta and Harrison were saying simple, traditional vows now, and Sarah tried desperately to listen.

Tears still streamed down her face, and she had to sniffle to keep her nose from running.

She was a mess. She was a fool. She was horribly embarrassed.

She saw a motion farther down the pew. Ben's mother had reached for her purse and was pulling something out of it. She handed it to Ben, who was sitting beside her.

Ben handed it to Sarah.

A tissue.

Sarah accepted it gratefully, mopping up her face. She must look like a wreck, all her makeup smeared off.

She'd thought she'd been so pretty today too.

She leaned against Jonathan's side, feeling sheltered beneath his arm. It felt like he was taking care of her. Maybe he was.

Harrison was kissing his bride now, and Marietta was glowing like the sunshine. And the ceremony was over as they were all introduced to the newly married couple.

Sarah had finally managed to stop crying.

She ducked her head against Jonathan's shoulder as they got up and walked to the narthex. She didn't want Ben or anyone to ask what had been wrong with her.

She didn't have any sort of answer, except the wedding had felt real to her in a way weddings never had before.

The next hour passed in a haze. They had to stay for some photographs—fortunately not too many since they weren't part of the bridal party. Sarah went to the restroom to restore her face with a paper towel. She needed to touch up her makeup, which she hadn't brought with her, and her hair was slipping out of the chignon, but otherwise she decided she didn't look too bad.

The reception was back in the ballroom of the estate, spilling out onto the terrace and formal gardens. Jonathan had his hand on her back again as they entered the mansion, guiding her toward the reception. But she stopped. "Do you think I can run upstairs real quick and fix my makeup?"

Jonathan blinked. "Sure. I'll wait for you here."

"No, no." She felt silly enough as it was, and she didn't want to make a big deal about her makeup touch-ups. "You go on. I'll find you."

He nodded. He still hadn't asked her what had made her cry.

He probably never would.

She ran upstairs to her room, reapplied makeup, tried to smooth down her hair, and was on her way down the hall again in less than five minutes.

She nearly ran into Ben on the stairs.

"Hey," she said, "What are you doing?"

"I had to get away for a minute," he admitted. "Too many people."

She peered up at him curiously, figuring the crowds must be too hard on him emotionally because of his history with his family.

"You all right?" he asked, studying her face with his very dark eyes. "What was the breakdown about?"

"It wasn't a breakdown," she insisted. "It was nothing. Weddings make me emotional." It was a lie, but he would have no way of knowing that.

"Hmm," he said like he didn't believe her. Then he arched his eyebrows. "I thought maybe you were upset about losing your ring."

She stared up at him blankly. "What?"

"Your engagement ring." He nodded toward her left hand.

She looked down at it. Her ring finger was empty.

It took a minute for it to process, but when it did she gasped with a flare of panic. "My ring! What happened to it?"

"I don't know. You didn't have it on earlier today either. It didn't appear as though you and Jonathan had broken up your fake engagement, so I assumed you'd lost it or forgotten to put it on."

Sarah wracked her brain, trying to remember when she'd last been aware of it. She'd only worn the thing for a week, and so she wasn't used to keeping track of it, but it was unforgivable to lose something so expensive.

"Maybe it's just in your room," Ben suggested.

"Yes. Probably." She grabbed his arm. "Please help me look. I'm supposed to go down and meet Jonathan, and I don't want him to see it's missing."

Ben came along, agreeably enough, although he seemed to think the situation was amusing rather than urgent.

They looked on all the surfaces and the floor of the bedroom, bathroom, and closet. But the ring wasn't there.

When they'd finished searching, Sarah was almost in tears again. That ring was the most beautiful piece of jewelry she'd ever seen. She'd loved it. And she knew Jonathan must have paid a lot for it.

It wasn't even really hers. How could she have lost it?

"Don't start to panic yet," Ben said. "Try to calm down and think. When was the last time you noticed it?"

His reasonable tone struck her as rather obnoxious, but she knew he was right. She made herself close her eyes and breathe.

Then she remembered. "Damn. I was fiddling with it yesterday in the secret garden before I fell asleep."

"And you didn't see it afterward?"

She shook her head.

"Then that's where it is."

She glanced down nervously, as if she could see through to the ballroom on the floor beneath them. "What am I going to tell Jonathan?"

"Don't tell him anything. It's a madhouse down there. No one will know we've gone to look."

"You'll come with me?"

"Sure. Why not? Besides, it's dark and the gates are open. You shouldn't wander alone by yourself."

Feeling better, she and Ben went downstairs, and instead of heading to the ballroom, they turned into another hall. Ben had put his hand on her back as they got to the bottom of the stairs, but it didn't feel nice and protective like when Jonathan did it. It felt like he was discreetly hurrying her along.

She didn't care. It was nice that Ben was helping her at all. She was particularly glad because he paused to grab something from a utility closet. A flashlight.

She wouldn't have even thought about that.

The several minutes it took to walk to the garden only made Sarah more urgent and impatient. And the minutes it took to search the grass and beds around the hammock she'd been sleeping on yesterday were even worse.

They didn't find the ring immediately, and in the dark it was hard to see anything at all. Ben aimed the flashlight, but it only lit up a limited section of ground.

Getting more and more nervous, Sarah hiked up her skirt and knelt on the ground beneath the hammock. It had to be here somewhere.

"There!" she exclaimed, catching a glint as Ben moved the flashlight across the grass. "Point back here."

Ben knelt on the grass too and aimed the flashlight where she'd indicated.

The ring was there, mostly hidden in the soft grass.

She leaned over to grab it, ignoring how inelegant she must look on her hands and knees in the grass.

The hand she was bracing herself with slipped on the grass as she grabbed the ring, and she almost fell on her face. She would have fallen had Ben not reached out to grab her waist.

They were trying to extricate themselves from the awkward tangle when lights suddenly went on all around them.

They both blinked in surprise. Evidently there were landscape lights in the garden, which neither of them had even thought to look for.

Sarah was squinting toward the entrance to discover who'd turned them on when a familiar voice bellowed in a very unfamiliar tone. *"What the hell are you doing?"*

Ben managed to stand up, and he helped Sarah to her feet as well before he turned toward his cousin. "No need to overreact," he began, in a bland voice that would be like a slap in the face to someone who was angry.

Jonathan was definitely angry. He strode over to where they stood, practically shaking with pent rage. "Overreact? *Overreact?*"

Sarah was flabbergasted. She'd never seen Jonathan openly express anger before, and she'd certainly never seen him on the verge of implosion as he was now.

Ridiculously, something about the raw power of his anger stirred a response inside her. An emotional one. And a physical one.

She felt shaky so she reached out to grab something. It happened to be Ben's arm.

Evidently, this was a mistake. Jonathan made a sound in his throat—one that sounded strangely like a growl—and he grabbed her wrist to pull her hand away from his cousin's arm.

Sarah gaped at him.

"If you're going to sneak away to fuck, you could at least try to be more discreet," Jonathan gritted out. "If I saw you leave, others could see too."

Suddenly, Sarah realized what Jonathan had thought, why he was so angry. Maybe it had looked bad, she and Ben slipping away in the dark together. They'd both been on their knees in the grass, his arm around her waist.

Jonathan's assumption wasn't an entirely unreasonable one.

But still...

"Damn, man, you're an idiot," Ben muttered.

Jonathan stiffened visibly, his dark eyes glinting in the soothing landscape lighting. "I shouldn't be angry that you're here screwing my fiancée?"

"We both know she's not your fiancée."

"Ben," Sarah said reproachfully. He was saying exactly the wrong thing to calm Jonathan down. She had to assume he wasn't trying to. "Jonathan, I can see how you misinterpreted it, but we weren't—"

"What do you mean you know she's not my fiancée?" Jonathan interrupted, glaring between Sarah and Ben. He must have decided who to fix his anger on, because he turned to Sarah. "You told him?"

"No," she insisted, her voice wobbly. Not because she was scared of Jonathan but because she was so affected by his angry intensity. "I didn't tell him. He figured it out on his own. But would you please listen? We weren't doing anything."

"You weren't on your hands and knees in the dark with your dress pushed up?" Jonathan's words were curt, bitter. He was obviously trying to control his eruption of anger. Not to calm himself down but to ensure he remained in control of this encounter.

Ben had obviously had enough. He made a gesture of surrender. "Look, I think you're a fucking idiot, but this is between you and her. If you want to come find me and beat me to a pulp later, I'll be around."

Then he just walked away.

"Ben," she called after him, not even sure why she did. He didn't really need to be here since the main issue, as he'd said, was between her and Jonathan. But now she was alone with Jonathan.

A Jonathan whose coiled tension and endless patience had finally snapped.

She turned to look at him. He'd still been holding her wrist, but now he moved his hand up to grip her upper arm.

"He can leave," Jonathan gritted out. "You're the one who betrayed me."

She gasped in indignation, her shakiness and anxiety transforming to hot resentment in an instant. "*What?* You think I betrayed you?"

"What would you call it then? You're supposed to be my fiancée, and at the first opportunity, you run off to screw my cousin?"

"I'm not your fiancée," she practically screamed, trying to get through to his infuriating, pigheaded brain. "We aren't in a relationship. I can screw whomever I want."

This was really beside the point and not the best way to calm Jonathan down either. She knew that instinctively, but she was so frustrated she didn't even care.

How dare he confront her like this, acting as though she'd done something wrong, when all she'd ever done was be faithful to him?

"You're at least supposed to *pretend* you're my fiancée this week. That was our agreement." His voice was thick now with a new kind of emotion. "And you've done a pitifully poor job of keeping it." His hand tightened on her arm bruisingly, although she could tell it was unintentional.

"You're hurting me," she said, shaking her arm in his grip.

He dropped it like she'd burned him. "Sorry."

"I didn't screw Ben," she said, rubbing her arm where he'd grabbed her. "I had no intention of screwing Ben. He was helping me find my ring." She showed him the ring she'd had in her fist the whole time. "*Your* ring," she corrected.

He stared down at it, panting, intensity still radiating off him in waves.

"But I could screw Ben if I wanted to. You have no claim on me."

"I have no claim on you?" he repeated, his raspy tone making it a question.

"You're my boss," she said, the truth in the words aching. She said them anyway. "You're my boss. Nothing else. I can screw whomever I want."

He could counter the words if he wanted. He could say she was wrong, that she was more to him than an assistant. She desperately wanted him say something, to pick up the gauntlet her words had thrown down.

He stared at her for a long time, his dark eyes smoldering with something she didn't understand. Then, before she could prepare herself, he took her face in both of his hands and kissed her.

The kiss was hard, urgent, passionate—nothing gentle or patient about it. And she was so stunned that at first she couldn't even respond. Her hands fisted in the jacket of his tux as his mouth moved against hers roughly, and she just hung on.

He broke off the kiss suddenly, panting even harder as he stared down at her face again. Then he took a clumsy step back, as if he'd just realized what he'd done.

"Jonathan?" she asked, her voice breaking on the word.

Something was shuddering inside her now— something other than the anger, anxiety, and confusion that were also present.

Something that felt like hope.

Jonathan wasn't indifferent to her. He couldn't be. If he was, he wouldn't have snapped for the first time in years because he thought she was screwing his cousin.

He cared about her as a person. She'd always known that. He fixed the wheels on her chair and stocked her supply of peppermint balls.

But he must feel even more than that. He *must*.

Maybe he wanted her the same way she wanted him.

"Jonathan?" she asked again, reaching out to grip the lapels of his jacket. Then her question turned into a demand. "Tell me what you want."

He didn't tell her. He didn't say anything. But he reached out and pulled her into another kiss.

This time, she responded.

~

As Jonathan felt Sarah respond to his kiss, he was slammed with waves of desire and primal possessiveness. She was his. It felt like she was *his*.

He slid his fingers into her hair, accidentally dislodging the pins and causing her hair to spill down over his hand. He made a guttural sound of satisfaction and tangled his hand in her loose waves.

Her body had softened against his, her mouth had opened to the advance of his tongue. Her fingers were clawing eager lines into his back and shoulders as he deepened the kiss.

167

Her responsiveness thrilled him, and his mind turned into a hot buzz of excitement, pleasure, and lust.

"Jon-athan," she gasped, as they finally broke the kiss. He couldn't let her go though. He trailed a hungry line of kisses along her jaw and then down her neck. He sucked on the throbbing pulse in her throat.

She cried out softly in pleasure, squirming against him now. She wanted him. He could feel how much she wanted him in her body, in her hands, in her intensifying vocal responses.

He wanted to tell her how much he wanted her, but the only word that came out was her name, muffled by his lips on her skin.

She whimpered in response as if she'd understood him.

He tried to caress her all over, feeling the thin silk over all her lush curves, but their embrace faltered, and then her knees buckled, and they both ended up on the ground.

He didn't care. He moved over her, pulling one of her breasts out of her neckline so he could take it between his lips.

She arched up into his mouth, gasping raggedly and gripping his hair with both hands. "Yes. Please!"

Her obvious desire fueled his own urgency. He was almost painfully aroused now, trying not to grind himself too hard against her thigh. He mouthed and fondled her breasts for as long as he could bear, until she was writhing beneath him and begging him for more.

He reared up, panting as he stared down at her, flushed, tousled, and decadent in her vintage choker and discomposed dress. She wasn't just beautiful—she was real, alive, passionate, Sarah. He couldn't believe he'd been so angry with her just a few minutes ago. He had no idea what he'd ever do without her.

She must have seen something on his face because her wriggling stilled and her eyes were suddenly soft and thoughtful. "You okay?"

He nodded, reaching out to cup her cheek with one hand.

She covered his hand on her cheek with one of her own in a strangely intimate gesture of affection. Then she pumped her hips up to rub her groin against his. "Good. Then hurry up."

He choked on a huff of laughter and pushed her skirt up even more, his erection pulsing dangerously when he saw she wore only the flimsiest of white lace thongs beneath it. She was wearing another pair of the lace-topped stockings, and the effect was so sexy he was afraid he might embarrass himself.

Incongruously, she blushed an even deeper shade of red as he stared down at her, but her mouth twitched with amusement as she explained, "It's not my normal underwear. Had to avoid a panty line."

"Naturally," he agreed soberly, making her laugh again.

She pulled him down into another kiss, which quickly grew urgent. She clawed at his jacket, but it was too much of a pain to take off, so he didn't bother. Evidently realizing it wasn't worth the trouble, her hands moved down to the front of his pants. They were still kissing, their tongues thrusting against each other with the same rhythm of their rocking together.

Sarah fumbled with the button on his pants until she undid it. Then she fumbled some more until she was able to free his erection. She held him in one hand, trapped between their bodies, and it felt so good Jonathan heard himself groaning into her mouth.

He wanted to please her, wanted to go down on her, wanted to take his time and make sure he gave her as much as he possibly could. But his need was too great. He'd never last that long, and she seemed just as hungry and desperate since she kept grinding herself against him.

She tore her mouth away from his and rasped, "Jonathan, please. I need you *now*."

With another moan, he slipped a hand down to feel her intimately, something wanting to howl inside him when he felt how hot and wet she was. He adjusted his position so he could line himself up at her entrance, and then he nudged before he started to slide in.

He breathed deeply, trying to slow himself down, but Sarah wouldn't let him. She lifted her pelvis with a whimper, trying to complete the thrust. He pulled back and entered her again, fitting himself into her body until he was fully inside.

She felt so good—so hot and tight and wet and sweet—that his vision blurred and he felt a stirring in his balls. She clawed at his shoulders and wriggled against the penetration in a way that threatened his control even more.

"Jon-athan," she breathed. "So good, so good."

He wanted to respond, but all he could choke out was, "Sarah." His arms shook as he fought for control. He needed to please her. Couldn't let go too soon.

"No." She'd somehow known what he was thinking. "No, I want you like this. Take what you need. It's what I need too."

He muffled a groan and kissed her again, and then he couldn't control anything. His hips were moving of their own accord, pumping into her with short, fast thrusts. She tried a couple of times to wrap her legs around his waist, but when she did she tightened them on each thrust in a way that just intensified the pleasure. Soon he had to break the kiss. And then he had to readjust, straightening his arms so he could thrust from a better angle.

Her whimpers and moans turned to loud sobbing sounds of pleasure, and he could feel her body tightening beneath him.

His was tightening too. He was sweating beneath his tux, and her beautiful dress was pushed up in a messy bunch around her waist. They were supposed to be at the reception right now. Someone would notice their absence.

But he didn't care. He didn't care about anything but Sarah and how desperately he needed her, how desperately she needed him.

Their bodies slapped together with each thrust, making a carnal, inelegant sound, and a thread of concern made its way into his mind that he was being too hard, too rough. He tried to rein himself in, slowed down, eased the force of his thrusting. But Sarah made another sob—this one of frustration—and dug her fingernails into his ass. "More. I need more."

She wanted this. She wanted him. So he started to grunt with the rhythm of his thrusting.

He'd never made so much noise during sex before. He wasn't sure what had possessed him, but it couldn't be stopped.

He could feel her channel tightening around him as she approached orgasm, could feel all the muscles in her body tense in expectation.

Then she arched up with a loud cry as her body shuddered with her release. There was no way he could hold back his own climax after that. He made a low, uninhibited sound as he came hard, all the tension cresting like a wave.

It was so strong, so deep, he was leveled afterward. He fell down on top of her, gasping and exhausted. His hips kept giving little jerks as lingering tremors of pleasure ran through him. She would sometimes shake too.

When he could finally lift his head and ease some of his weight off her, he was hit with knowledge that was like a punch in the gut.

She was crying silently, tears streaming down the sides of her face and into her hair. As he watched, her shoulders shook with it.

He'd known he was out of control, but he'd thought they were together in it. He'd thought she'd wanted it as much as he had.

But maybe he'd been wrong.

CHAPTER TEN

Sarah didn't know what was wrong with her, but she was tired of all this crying. She'd never been a big crier, and there was no reason for her to start now.

As she'd climaxed though, as her body and heart had found such release, her eyes had followed suit. And now she was lying beneath a hot, relaxed, gasping, delicious Jonathan, blubbering like an idiot.

"What's wrong?" he asked, his flushed, sated face tightening into confusion and concern. "Did I hurt you?"

She shook her head, unable to speak over the lump in her throat.

"Sarah, tell me what's wrong. I would have stopped." His expression twisted as if he momentarily doubted his words. Then, "I'm sure I could have stopped. I thought you wanted this too."

"I did," she managed to choke. "I do. I know you would have stopped. I didn't want you to."

"Then why are you crying."

"I've just been crying for no reason all day," Sarah admitted. "Once I got started, I couldn't stop."

Her words were true, but as she tried to wipe her wet face with her fingers, she started to get an inkling of why she was so emotional to begin with.

She'd never been in love before. Not for real. Not like this. And swinging between poles of giddy excitement and impending heartache was evidently quite a strain on one's emotional equilibrium.

Jonathan gazed down at her, that questioning concern still on his face. His bow tie was askew, and his hair was rumpled with perspiration and all the tugging she'd done, so it was sticking out in all directions. He was hot and heavy on top of her, and she was uncomfortably wet between her legs from his release and hers.

But she would be more than happy to live this moment over and over again for the rest of her life.

He adjusted his arms so he could swipe at one of her tears with his thumb. It looked like he was going to say something—maybe something she really wanted to hear—so she waited, her breath caught in her throat.

After a minute, he glanced away—down at her lips. Then he leaned down to kiss them very gently.

She let out her breath as she kissed him back. The kiss was very nice. She reached up to hold the back of his neck and caress his just slightly bristly jaw with her palm.

But she would have rather he said something.

He'd never been a forthcoming man though. And she knew—she *knew*—he wouldn't be kissing her now, not so tenderly, not like this, if he didn't have some kind of feelings for her.

He was a man who showed his feelings. Maybe it would just take him more time to get the words said.

He eventually deepened the kiss, and Sarah couldn't help but respond. She'd just had a powerful orgasm, but she felt an ache of arousal tighten between her legs again as Jonathan stroked the inside of her mouth with his tongue.

She was breathing in fast little pants when he broke the kiss to trail his mouth down her throat, his bristles scratching the sensitive skin there.

"Jon-athan," she gasped, arching up slightly against his weight. "We need to go back to the reception."

"Mm-hmm." It sounded like agreement, but he was sucking her pulse and one of his hands had slipped down to stroke her hip.

"I don't want to go all turned on like this." She had a fistful of his hair, and she told herself she was trying to pull his head up from her neck. Instead, she was involuntarily holding his head in place.

"You won't be turned on when we go," he murmured thickly. He'd moved down to her breasts, taking one in his mouth and fondling the other with his hand.

Sarah arched up even higher at the sensations. "Jon-Jonathan," she tried again. "I am turned on. Right now."

"I can take care of that."

"What are you doing?" she asked, shifting with deepening arousal as he caressed her. "We already had—oh God!—sex."

"I feel like I came too soon," he explained, mouthing her belly through the thin silk of her dress. "Should make up for it."

"What do you mean? I came. It was great."

"I know." Despite what sounded like agreement, he didn't stop his slow trip down her body. Eventually, he sat up higher to stroke up her thighs with both hands until he'd reached her now-pulsing arousal.

"Jon-athan!" she cried, when he penetrated her with two fingers, despite the wet evidence of their earlier intercourse. "What... what are..." She couldn't finish the question because he'd leaned down to flick his tongue against her clit.

She closed her eyes against the intense sensations, arching up again and again as his skillful fingers and mouth worked her up toward climax.

"Oh God, oh God, oh God," she mumbled as an orgasm tightened inside her. She fumbled for purchase on the ground but only came away with handfuls of grass.

She cried out as she came hard and then kept crying out as he didn't stop. His fingers pushed into her G-spot, and he alternated sucking and flicking her clit.

She came again hard. At some point, she'd hooked her legs around his shoulders, and he was having to fight to keep from being strangled between her thighs as he worked her over, bringing her to one more orgasm.

She collapsed on the grass limply when he finally raised his head, wiping his mouth with the back of his hand in a strangely primitive gesture.

"Oh, God, Jonathan," she gasped. "How did you do that?"

He chuckled, although his dark eyes were soft and hot as he gazed down at her. "I've always been good at anatomy."

She couldn't help but laugh, her chest hurting with the swell of affection. "We do need to get back. I don't want to offend your uncle or hurt Harrison and Marietta's feelings."

"Yeah," he agreed, heaving himself to his feet and quickly tucking in his shirt and fastening his trousers.

His tux was rather wrinkled, and his skin was covered with a sheen of perspiration. His hair needed to be smoothed down. He looked absolutely scrumptious.

He extended a hand to help her to her feet, and she cringed as she adjusted her clothing. "I'm a mess."

"No, you're not," he said, helping her pull down her skirt in the back.

"I can't go to the reception like this." Her dress wasn't wrinkled as badly as she'd feared. It must be some sort of miracle fabric. But she felt, and no doubt looked and smelled, like she'd been fucked hard in the grass. "Do I have grass stains on my butt?"

"No. Just on your back here." He wiped at her dress just between her shoulder blades, as if that could remove grass stains.

"I can cover that with my sweater." She put on the little cardigan she'd dropped earlier. "But I'll need to do some work on everything else. My hair must be a wreck."

"It's not." He was looking at her now, her messy hair, her hot face, her mussed dress, like she was beautiful, like he loved the sight of it.

Sarah almost melted.

To distract herself from the feelings, she looked around on the grass. "I need my ring. I dropped it earlier. It must be around here somewhere."

He helped her look and found it a minute later. He lifted her left hand and slid it on her ring finger.

He'd been focused on her hand as he put on the ring, but now he lifted his eyes to her face.

Her breath hitched at the look in his eyes, and her hand in his started to tremble.

It felt real. Like he meant it. And it looked again like he would say something.

He did. "We better get going."

~

They returned to the estate, and Sarah ran upstairs to her room to rescue her appearance. She cleaned herself up and redid her hair and makeup. She was tempted to change her dress, but she knew people would notice that. Plus she didn't really have anything else to wear appropriate for this particular wedding reception.

So she smoothed out the wrinkles as best she could, made sure the grass stain was covered by her cardigan, and decided she didn't look too debauched.

She went down to the ballroom to find Jonathan.

It hadn't even been an hour—despite how much seemed to have happened since they'd gotten back from the ceremony—and guests were still mingling over cocktails before the dinner started.

She couldn't find Jonathan. She eventually asked Gordon, who said he'd just seen him go into an anteroom off the ballroom.

Sarah went to the room Gordon indicated and found Jonathan and Ben in conversation.

Conversation might have been stretching it, since they were just staring at each other stoically when she walked in.

"You guys aren't fighting, are you?" She walked over to stand next to Jonathan, looking between the two men in concern.

"He thinks I'm an asshole," Ben said, half smiling at her through his beard.

"Well, you are." She returned Ben's half smile so he would know there wasn't any teeth in her remark, but then cut her eyes back to Jonathan. "But I do think it can go unsaid."

Jonathan narrowed his eyes but didn't say anything. He still was really angry at Ben, she could see, despite the great sex he'd just had.

"Did you all work things out?" Ben asked, evidently noticing their exchanged look. "I hate to see a fake engagement fall apart."

"And that's another thing," Jonathan said. "If Sarah didn't tell you, how the hell did you know we aren't really engaged?"

"Excuse me." The words were clipped and cold, and the new voice sliced through their conversation like a razor. "You aren't engaged?"

Sarah gasped, and they all turned to see Cyrus Damon, standing in the doorway of the anteroom.

Jonathan froze, and Sarah's heart started to race. Ben's features twisted briefly, maybe with annoyance, maybe with concern.

"I was just playing around," Ben said, in an admirably convincing attempt to keep their whole ruse from collapsing. "Teasing Sarah."

It didn't work, of course. This was Cyrus Damon, and he'd never in his life been manipulated. "I heard the entire conversation." His eyes bored into Jonathan's. "Your engagement is fake?"

Jonathan opened his mouth to respond, but his uncle wouldn't let him. He pressed on, so frigidly it made Sarah shiver. "I think I understand. You were so concerned with the funding of your little lab that you were willing to deceive your family and take advantage of this young woman? Very nicely done."

"Sir," Sarah put in, her whole body shaking now in anxiety and her instinctive dislike of conflict. "He didn't take advantage of me. And we really didn't—"

"I appreciate your loyalty to him," Cyrus said. "But he is your employer, and thus he has power over you. This is his responsibility, and one he has evidently failed at utterly."

Sarah made a choked sound at how much these words would hurt Jonathan.

Jonathan didn't react though. He just stood perfectly still, staring at his uncle.

"And evidently, he is also willing to betray his family."

"No," Sarah objected, too upset to know the most strategic response in this situation. "It wasn't like that. We really didn't mean—"

"I don't blame you, my dear," Cyrus said, as perfectly civil and courteous as he ever was. His chocolate brown eyes—just like Harrison's—iced up when he flicked them back to Jonathan. "My nephew is the one to blame."

Sarah was almost in tears—at the transformation of a kind, old-fashioned man into a stone-cold tyrant and at the retreat she saw in Jonathan's face, liked he'd buried himself deeply inside himself.

He'd only just started to come out.

But she hadn't forgotten about Ben, whose face had grown angrier as his uncle continued the verbal assault.

He met her eyes, and for a moment, she saw a sympathy so deep it made her ache.

But then he looked back at his uncle, and his expression tightened into angry impatience. He opened his mouth to say something.

Cyrus cut him off. "We will not have this conversation now. We will not ruin this occasion with such immaturity and selfishness. We can speak tomorrow."

Jonathan still didn't say anything.

Ben made a slight gesture with his hands—almost one of surrender—and he turned on his heel to walk out of the anteroom.

Sarah was quite sure that Ben would also walk out of the ballroom, out of the house, out of his family's estate.

And he wouldn't come back.

~

Jonathan stared down at his half-filled suitcase, dazed and unable to move.

He wasn't sure how or why everything had fallen apart so quickly, but he was having trouble keeping up with it.

He'd been wrong to lie to his family. He knew that, although it had initially seemed like a reasonable plan.

But he'd just started to feel at home with them, feel like they were people who might like him, even when he hadn't accomplished enough. He'd actually been thinking on his way back to the house from the garden with Sarah that he should probably tell them the truth and accept the consequences to his lab.

It was a moot point now. He'd been a fool. His uncle was never going to love him. He would never do anything good enough for that.

Sarah was downstairs with the others, giving Harrison and Marietta their sendoff of flung birdseed and happy cheers. He could hear them, but he couldn't join them.

When Harrison discovered the truth, he would react exactly like their uncle.

Jonathan had managed to go back and get the rest of his shirts from the closet and was starting to fold them haphazardly in the suitcase when Sarah entered the room.

She stared at him for a minute, obviously processing what he was doing. "You're not even going to talk to them?" she asked at last.

He shook his head in a slight gesture, since it seemed rude not to respond at all, and kept folding his shirts.

"Jonathan," Sarah said softly. She came over to sit on the edge of the bed, idly pulling out the pins and shaking her hair loose. "He was angry and surprised. But if you talk, you can probably work things out. Just explain what really happened."

"He knows what really happened," Jonathan managed to say, even though his throat hurt as if from disuse. "He's not going to change his mind." When she looked like she was going to argue, he continued, "I know him better than you do."

"But what about the others? Harrison and Andrew and Marietta and Laurel? They've been nothing but nice to us, and to leave without a word to them..."

"You're welcome to talk to them," he said, not looking at her because her big anxious eyes and wobbling mouth bothered him so much.

She didn't respond immediately. Just sat and looked at him as he folded shirts. Then finally, "I thought you were starting to like them."

He *had* been starting to like them. "I'm going to leave tonight."

"I don't really think you have to. He hasn't asked you to leave, and I think if you talk and explain everything to him, he might understand."

"You don't know him like I do."

She paused again, as if she were thinking deeply or else working up the nerve to say what she wanted to say. "I don't think you know him as well as you think."

He was angry then—not as much at her as at the fact that she believed her words were true. "Less than a year ago, he didn't talk to Harrison for two months because he disapproved of his relationship with Marietta. You think he'll be more accepting of the fact that I lied to him and tried to trick him into funding the lab?"

"Maybe not," she admitted, ducking her head and hiding her face behind the curtain of her hair. "But I don't think I was totally wrong about him. When I talked to him, he really wanted to get closer to you. I wasn't wrong about that. He loves you, you know."

Jonathan shook her head, staring down at his folded clothes in the suitcase. "I understand why you want to believe that. Your family loves you, and so you can't imagine a world in which they didn't. My family just isn't like that."

He cleared his throat. "I'm leaving tonight, but you don't have to come with me. You're welcome to stay. No one is angry at you."

Sarah made a choked sound. "Of course I'm coming with you. What do you think… Surely you know I'm on *your* side in this."

He let out a short breath and closed his suitcase.

Sarah stood up and grabbed his arm. "You know that, right?"

He managed to grit out, "Thanks." It felt like there was a clamp around his chest, like it was suffocating him. He just wanted to breathe normally but couldn't seem to do so. "We can stay in London tonight and fly out tomorrow, if that's okay."

She nodded. "I can get packed quickly. I might say good-bye to everyone, if that's okay with you. They were nice to me. I… I liked them."

Her voice broke on the penultimate word, and Jonathan shot her an instinctive look of concern. Her face twisted briefly, but she smiled at him. "If you want to leave sooner, you could throw my stuff in the bags, and I'll run down now and say good-bye."

He told her this was fine and went to the closet to get her largest suitcase. He tried to pack her stuff as neatly as he could, but it all looked so pretty and delicate he wasn't sure he did a good job. It felt strange—intimate—to pack her underwear and stockings. A few minutes later, a footman arrived to help him haul the bags to the car.

They'd loaded the car when he came back into the hallway. He heard familiar voices in the parlor, so he automatically paused to listen.

"Why did he give me a note?" Sarah said. He couldn't see her but he could hear her voice clearly.

She must be talking to Gordon because the butler replied, "I'm afraid I can't answer that, miss."

"Does Mr. Damon know we're leaving?"

"Yes, miss."

"And he's really not going to come out to talk to Jonathan?" Sarah's voice held a surprised hurt that made Jonathan's chest ache even more.

He'd known what to expect. And she hadn't.

"I'm afraid I can't say, miss," Gordon replied, as perfectly discreet as ever. "Perhaps you might read the note for more explanation."

There was a pause, during which Sarah must have read the note. Jonathan knew he shouldn't be eavesdropping, but he felt awkward about showing himself since they were talking about him.

"He says he greatly enjoyed meeting me and I'm welcome at the manor anytime. He is sorry it ended the way it did. He doesn't say anything about Jonathan. Should I go try to talk to him, do you think?"

"I wouldn't advise that, miss. He isn't entertaining company this evening."

"I don't understand. Jonathan is his nephew. If they would just talk, I'm sure they could work it out. I thought he—" She stumbled over her words, sounding like she was swallowing over tears. "He's intimidating, but I really did like him."

There was silence from the parlor for several long seconds. Then Gordon finally said, "My family had a dog when I was a boy."

"Oh." Sarah sounded confused, off stride. She wouldn't know Gordon's absolute loyalty to Cyrus Damon. He would never dream of saying a word against his employer or speaking inappropriately on private family matters. "Did you?"

"He was an ornery creature and barked relentlessly at anyone who came close to the house."

"One of our dogs was like that." Sarah still sounded like she wasn't sure of the point of this conversation, but she would never be rude or show disinterest in someone else.

"I was very young, and I was terrified of that dog. The barking was so loud, and he would snarl and show his teeth. I was sure he would attack and hurt me."

"Did he ever bite you?"

"No. My mother kept telling me that he only barked that way because he was trying to protect the family, and he didn't really know how to behave around people. She said I needed to trust the dog, get close enough so I could pet him—and then he'd be my best friend."

"And did you?" Sarah sounded breathless now, as if she'd figured out the point of Gordon's story at the same time that Jonathan did as he listened.

"Yes. That dog was my best friend for eleven years."

Jonathan walked away, back outside to where the car was waiting. And Sarah came out a few minutes later with Andrew.

Andrew wasn't smiling—which was so uncharacteristic of the man that it caused a stab of guilt to slice through him. He and Andrew had never been close, but he still felt like an ass for lying to him.

"Sarah explained what happened," Andrew said as they approached. "We understand. I called Harrison too. It's his wedding night, so he's a little distracted, but he's not angry either." He glanced back at the looming, dignified Georgian mansion behind them. "Lord Uncle will get over it. He always does." He extended a hand to Jonathan. "Keep in touch. I mean it. You and Sarah should come visit me and Laurel at the inn. Santorini would be like heaven after Iceland."

Jonathan shook the hand Andrew offered. "Thanks." He wasn't sure what else to say, since so much had been packed into his cousin's words. But he was glad Harrison and Andrew at least weren't resentful of the lies they'd told.

Sarah didn't look surprised or flustered at Andrew's assumption that they'd be vacationing together, even though he knew they weren't really engaged. She kissed Andrew on the cheek, and then she and Jonathan got in the back of the chauffeured car.

They drove in mostly silence to London. It was late, and Sarah was tired. She leaned against him in the backseat and seemed to doze off after a half hour or so.

They checked into a hotel, and because Jonathan wasn't thinking, he just got a room with a king-sized bed. Sarah didn't seem surprised though. She just put down her bag and pulled her phone out of her purse. Glancing at her watch, she said, "I might call my parents if that's all right."

He wasn't sure why she was checking with him. She could do anything she wanted. "Of course."

She went out to the balcony to make her phone call in privacy, and Jonathan took a shower and got into bed since he felt absolutely battered.

Sarah came back in after about a half hour. Jonathan had never talked to a member of his family on the phone for that long in his life. He wondered what she'd told them— about him, about all this. He didn't ask her, of course.

"I'm going to take a shower too," she said. "I feel kind of ick."

Jonathan could hardly believe they'd made love in the garden. Only a few hours ago. He left the light on beside Sarah's side of the bed but turned off the rest of them in the room. He lay in the dim room until she came out, wearing a little shorts-and-tank pajama set.

She turned off the light and crawled into bed beside him. He was on his side, facing away from her, but he could feel her eyes on him in the dark.

"Are you okay?" she asked at last.

He grunted, which was all the answer he could articulate.

She rolled over closer to him. He could feel the bed shift. "Did you want to talk about it?"

He did want to talk about it, but he couldn't. That would mean he'd have to say out loud that he'd failed, that he hadn't lived up, that nothing he'd ever done had been good enough.

"It's too hard a world," she said, very softly.

He didn't know what she was talking about, and he wanted to know. So he managed to grunt, "What?"

"It's too hard a world to live in. The one where you always have to earn your place."

He took a couple of shaky breaths. He suspected Sarah was still staring at his back, and this suspicion was confirmed when he felt her scoot even closer to him. Then her arms wrapped around him, and she was spooning him from behind.

"I don't want to live in that world," she murmured, just behind his shoulder.

He had to say something then. To tell her. To make sure she knew. To say the truth out loud. "Neither do I."

He heard her release a thick breath. "Then we won't."

She didn't say anything else, but he could feel care and sympathy in her arms, in her hands, in her soft little body.

He didn't sleep, and neither did she. Her hands would sometimes stroke his chest, his belly. After a long time, he found he could breathe naturally again. He took long inhales and exhales, and his body started to relax.

She kept caressing his chest, her fingers skimming over the hair, the nipples, the flat planes of his abdomen.

As he relaxed, he became more and more conscious of her body behind him pressed into his. Her breasts, her hair, her legs, her quiet breathing.

His chest still ached, but his body started to react to her embrace. When her hand trailed down to his stomach, he hardened even more.

He didn't move, didn't say anything. She was trying to comfort him. She wasn't coming onto him. Arousal was an inappropriate response to her care and concern.

But he couldn't hide it forever. Her stroking hand eventually found his erection. She caressed it gently, the same way she'd been caressing his chest and stomach. His pelvis bucked slightly into her hand, but he resisted the impulse to do any more.

When her massage became firmer, more intentional, he reached down to stop her.

"You don't want to?" she asked, sounding almost hurt.

He said thickly, "I do. But you can't possibly—"

"I do too," she murmured, beginning her massage of his erection again. "I want to too."

He smothered a groan and rolled over, settling between her legs. She wasn't as wet as she'd been on their previous times, but he could still slide into her pretty easily. Her breathing had accelerated, and so had his, and they rocked together in otherwise silence.

She didn't come—at least he didn't think she did. But she seemed to want this, want him anyway. And he desperately needed her care, her trust, her sweetness, her

body. His motion was clumsy and eager at the end, and his release was consuming.

He was limp and boneless afterward—not from fatigue as much as aftermath.

It was so hard for his brain to even process what had happened, what it revealed. That Sarah cared about him—deeply—even at his lowest point, when he'd done nothing to deserve it, nothing for her to admire or appreciate. Failed in every way.

In theory, he'd known such a thing existed, but it had never been part of his experience before.

Until now. Until Sarah.

He would made sure he answered it, answered her. He couldn't give her what she deserved yet. He was still her boss, and that made things a little tricky. But he would figure out some way to handle it—where she could keep her job and they could be together. He would make it work.

Then he would show her that he loved her with everything he had.

Their bodies were still entangled when he fell asleep. It was almost morning, but if it hadn't been for Sarah, he wouldn't have slept at all.

CHAPTER ELEVEN

Sarah woke up late. She was sure it was late, even before she opened her eyes. The first thing she heard was Jonathan's voice—a soft murmuring that was soothing in its familiarity.

She opened her eyes and saw that it was almost ten o'clock. She never slept so late.

Jonathan sat in a chair in the seating group by the window in the far corner. He was talking on the phone, his tablet on his lap.

She stretched under the covers to test how she felt. She was a little sore from sex—twice yesterday—and her head felt a little fuzzy, but that could be from the late night.

She sat up in bed, readjusting her camisole so one of her breasts wasn't hanging out.

Jonathan glanced over and obviously saw she was awake, but he didn't give any greeting. She could hear more of what he was saying now. He was trying to arrange a time to talk to someone.

She listened for a minute or two, then got up to get a cup of coffee from the pot Jonathan had evidently ordered from room service.

He was starting to get frustrated. She could hear it in his overly patient voice. Whomever he wanted to talk to evidently wasn't easy to contact.

She went over to check his travel mug on the table beside him. It was almost empty, so she went to fill it up.

He mouthed the word "thanks" as she handed it to him but didn't smile or meet her eyes.

She noticed his eyes flick briefly over her body. She must look a mess in her wrinkled pajamas and tangled hair. But his attention was clearly focused on the phone conversation.

She went back to sit on the side of the bed and sipped her coffee. When he hung up, clearly having been unsuccessful, she started to say good morning, but he immediately started to dial someone else from a number he read from his tablet.

When she heard him begin the conversation with whomever picked up, she realized what he was doing.

He was starting to make calls to potential funders of the lab, since his uncle was likely to pull out.

He'd never wanted to do this. She knew it would be hard for him. He didn't like to ask for help. He didn't want someone else to direct the course of his research and perhaps steer it off course because of money or politics. He'd been in the enviable and rare situation before of not having to do so.

But the lab was more important to him than his reluctance to hand over control.

He evidently had more luck with this conversation since he made an appointment for a phone conference the following day at three forty-five. When he hung up this time, he took a long sip of coffee, and his eyes strayed over to where she was sitting on the bed.

"Did I wake you up?" he asked at last.

"No. I don't think so. I needed to get up anyway."

"No hurry. Our flight home doesn't leave until six."

Since he was looking at her in a strange way, she didn't say anything. She waited, wondering if he was going to share how he felt, what he wanted to happen between them.

Surely it was time. She wasn't expecting for him to declare his endless love for her—although she certainly wouldn't complain if that happened. They'd had sex twice the day before, however, and their relationship had obviously changed.

She really needed to know what he was thinking.

She'd be happy to take it as slow as he wanted. She'd be happy just to hear how he felt.

She finished her coffee, and he still hadn't spoken. Her pulse was starting to throb in her throat.

"Have you heard from... from anyone? Your uncle?"

He shook his head as his only response. His shoulders were stiff beneath his T-shirt, and he hadn't yet shaved.

"Did...," she asked at last, after another long pause, her voice catching as she grew more and more nervous. "Did you want to talk?"

He shook his head, glancing back down to his tablet. "I've got all these calls to make."

She felt rebuffed and brutally disappointed. "Okay," she said, praying she sounded natural. She hid her face behind her hair as she put her coffee cup in the kitchenette, grabbed some clothes from her suitcase, and hurried toward the bathroom.

"Sarah," Jonathan said, just before she got there. His voice was so thick it stopped her.

She looked over her shoulder at him and saw he was walking toward her. She waited breathlessly.

"I'm sorry," he said, in that same thick voice. His features twisted briefly. "But I need to get this done."

She understood. Everything she needed to know.

He cared about her. Wanted her. But she'd never be as important to him as his work. He'd committed his whole life to work. That was where he'd always found the most fulfillment. So any sort of relationship with her would take a backseat to that.

And Sarah realized she just couldn't accept that.

Working with Jonathan was wonderful, and sex was even better. But she wanted—she needed—more from him.

He cared about her, but he didn't care enough. And there was no way for them to go back to the way things had been.

Even if Jonathan managed to find new funding for his lab, there was no way Sarah could keep working there.

She'd lost her dream job, after all, as sure as if he'd fired her.

She'd talked to her parents the night before. They'd put her on speaker phone, as usual, and her mother had kept asking if she was all right. She tried to sound upbeat, but she knew she hadn't succeeded. She hadn't said anything about what happened between her and Jonathan, but they weren't fools. They knew something was going on.

Her father had said, "You don't have to stay there. You don't have to keep working there."

"I know," she'd said in response. "But I need to wait and... and see what happens." Last night, she'd still had hope that Jonathan would tell her what she wanted to hear. That they could have a future.

"You can come home," her father kept repeating. "You can always come home. If you're not happy there, just come home until you find another job. You could find one here in the States. They'll snap you up right away. Anyone would be lucky to have you. Just come home if you're not happy there."

She'd been crying on the phone at that point, strangling herself to keep her parents from hearing.

It hadn't worked. Her mother said, "Oh, sweetie, please don't cry."

They loved her and wanted her closer. They always had, although they never once reproached her for moving so far away. They wanted her to be happy.

Sarah wanted to be happy too. She didn't want to spend morning after morning crying in the shower like this.

She knew what she was going to do. She would see what happened on the way home. If Jonathan had even the slightest intention of pursuing a real relationship with her, he would say something by then. But she wasn't holding out hope anymore. He'd already told her what she needed to know.

He had to get his work done.

When she got back, she would unpack her new clothes and pack up her old comfortable ones. She'd get a flight to New York and from there to Las Vegas. Her father would come to pick her up at the airport.

With her training and experience, she knew she could find another job very quickly. Pharmaceutical companies would pay her a fortune to work for them. It wasn't what she had always wanted, but it would be better than this.

She'd leave a note for Jonathan. She started to compose it in her mind. She couldn't let him see how heartbroken she was. He'd feel guilty. He'd feel responsible.

She would just leave and start over with her job, her career, her life, her heart.

Jonathan might not love her—no man ever really had—but her family always would.

It would be enough.

~

Jonathan knew he had hurt Sarah's feelings by postponing the conversation with her, but he couldn't bring himself to offer himself to her when he had absolutely nothing to offer.

He'd formulated a plan as he lay awake last night. He would find someone else to fund the lab—at least for a year. If he had to use his savings, what he'd inherited from his parents, until he secured alternate funding, then he would do that.

Then he would work out a new contract for her position, one where he was no longer her boss.

He couldn't offer Sarah any sort of future until he'd at least taken care of that.

Then, once he had more to show for himself—some sort of financial and career security for her—then he would see if she would accept his ring for real.

The thought gave him hope—like there was a way out of the dismal failure he'd been last night.

He was on the phone and e-mailing most of the day until their flight took off. And he spent the plane ride writing up a funding proposal to send to potential funders.

Sarah was quiet, but she didn't seem as upset as she had that morning. She knew him better than anyone. She would understand. He wanted her desperately—she knew how much—but he could be patient until he was in the situation to give her what she deserved.

When they got back to the lab, he didn't even unpack. Just went immediately to his office to make calls.

One of his calls was very successful, and—when he hung up—he was smiling. Nothing was certain yet, there would be a lot to work out, but he might have found funding for at least a year's operation of the lab. And it was from a private individual, which was far simpler than dealing with the hassles and red tape of a foundation or institution.

He wanted to tell Sarah. She would be as excited as he was. He reached for the phone to call her when he noticed he'd missed a call from the lab's security station. He dialed them back immediately since they only contacted him when there was a problem.

"This is Damon," he said, when the security guard picked up.

"Dr. Damon," the man said, "This is Peter. Sorry to bother you. I wasn't sure if I should or not."

"What's the problem?"

"It's not a problem, I don't think. But Dr. Stratford left her keys with me. I hadn't heard she was leaving, which isn't normal. So I just wanted to let you know."

Jonathan frowned. "What do you mean she left her keys?"

"Her keys. All of them. To her apartment, to the lab, to the buildings. All of them. She dropped them off with me when she left just now."

Jonathan started to feel the beginnings of a flare of panic. "She left? Where did she go? Did she take one of the cars?"

"No. She'd called a cab, and they picked her up. I don't know where she was going, but she had suitcases, so I assume she's heading to the airport."

Jonathan vision darkened for a moment, so intently was he trying to process this information. It was wrong. All of it was wrong. He felt that clamp in his chest again, but it was far more brutal now than it had been last night. "Meet me over at housing," he managed to say, "so you can let me into her apartment."

As he walked over in long, urgent strides, he dialed Sarah's cell. It rang several times, but then her voice mail picked up.

He glared down at the phone in frustration. Tried to dial her again. This time it went immediately to voice mail.

She wasn't going to answer a call from him.

He had no idea what was happening. Why would she leave? And without even a word?

He'd trusted her, thought she'd cared about him.

She must know how desperately he loved her.

Peter was waiting in front of Sarah's apartment when he arrived, looking nervous and confused.

"I'm so sorry, Dr. Damon," he said. "If I'd known she wasn't supposed to leave, I would have tried to stop her."

"It's not your fault," Jonathan muttered. "Just unlock it for me."

Peter opened the door and Jonathan burst into the apartment. It looked perfectly neat, but some of the personal items like framed photos and the Stanford sweatshirt that always hung on a hook near the door weren't there. The collection of the vampire show weren't there either.

He saw a folded piece of paper on the table. When he picked it up, he noticed it had been folded over the engagement ring he'd given her.

He stared down at the ring, dazed and disoriented.

Finally, his eyes focused enough to read the note.

I'm sorry to leave like this, but I think it's for the best. I'll arrange to have the rest of my stuff shipped if you can give me a week or two. I don't think I can work with you anymore after everything that's happened. But it's not your fault. Don't feel bad about anything. You're the best scientist and the best man I've ever known, and I'll always be grateful for everything you've taught me. Love, Sarah.

He stared down at the note blindly for way too long.

It didn't make sense. None of it made sense.

"Is something wrong, Dr. Damon?" Peter asked, sounding awkward and nervous.

"She's... she's left me."

"Oh." Peter was obviously bewildered about how to respond. "I'm sorry, sir. We all always thought..." He trailed off.

"Thought what?" Jonathan prompted, more to make conversation that sounded somewhat normal than because he really cared.

"We all thought you and she were a pair."

They had been a pair, a couple. For the past week, for the past three years. He couldn't even begin to process what his world would become without her in it.

She was... everything.

"Do you think you could maybe get her back? She only left about thirty minutes ago."

Jonathan looked at his watch without really seeing it, but he suddenly knew what he had to do. "Yes. Have someone pull a car around."

He balled up the note and left it on the table since he hated it and everything it represented. But he stuck the ring in his pocket as he strode out of the room.

He went to the front gate. Then he drove like a madman to the airport. He tried calling her several more times on this way, but she wouldn't pick up.

The Reykjavik airport wasn't large, but it wasn't easy to find one person there when he had no idea where she would be.

He made himself calm down enough to think. She would probably be going to her parents. He scanned the outbound flights, and the only one to the States that afternoon was a flight to New York. Surely that was what she'd be taking.

They wouldn't let him past security without a ticket, and the only seats available were first class, so he bought one.

He got bogged down in security, and by the time he made it to the gate, the passengers had already boarded.

He gave the woman his ticket and got on the plane, still not knowing if Sarah as actually on it.

He was the last passenger on board, and they wouldn't let him go back and search the seats in coach because they were preparing for takeoff.

So Jonathan took his seat, ready to strangle someone with his frustration and growing fear.

What if Sarah had decided she simply couldn't put up with a man as hopeless and inarticulate as he was? What if she just didn't want him anymore?

Why else would she have left?

He'd worked himself up into quite a state when the pilot finally turned off the fasten-seatbelt light. The elderly woman beside him kept eyeing him nervously, probably because he kept stewing and fidgeting and frowning.

He got up immediately, ignored the attendant's offer of help, and pushed aside the curtain separating first class from the rest of the plane.

He walked down the aisle into coach, scanning the passengers for Sarah's vivid hair and much-loved face.

He finally saw her in a back corner. She was leaning against the window, her face covered by her hair.

Jonathan breathed a sigh of relief and started back toward her.

No matter what, he was going to get her back. He loved her, and she was his.

CHAPTER TWELVE

The first obstacle was the middle-aged woman sitting in the seat next to Sarah. She was watching as Jonathan approached and was obviously startled when he crouched down so he was on her eye level.

The couple in the seats across the aisle and the young man in the seat in front of the woman turned to watch him too. Feeling awkward but determined, Jonathan nodded toward Sarah. "I need to talk to her."

Sarah had her eyes closed, but they flew open at the sound of his voice. She jerked in surprise and straightened up. "What are you doing here?" Her voice broke on the penultimate word.

"You left."

She frowned and didn't say anything, obviously too taken aback to form words.

"You left without saying anything." Jonathan would prefer to have this conversation in private, but he was the one who'd messed this up and so he was going to fix it—even if that meant spilling out his heart in front of a bunch of strangers.

"Wait," Sarah said, blinking. "You're on the plane?"

"It was the only way to catch up with you. They wouldn't let me get to the gate without a ticket, and then you'd already boarded."

She looked like she'd been crying, a fact that cut into his chest, and now a couple of tears streamed out of her eyes and down her cheeks. "But *why?*"

"Isn't it obvious, honey?" the middle-aged woman said. She was obviously American and spoke with a pronounced Southern accent. "He couldn't let you leave without telling you he loves you. No wonder you've been crying, poor thing."

"Well, let the man say it," the wife of the couple across the aisle put in. "You're interrupting his big moment."

Jonathan was torn between frustration and self-consciousness, and the combination paralyzed his tongue. He'd been planning out his whole declaration on the drive over, but now he couldn't remember any of it. He just stared at Sarah, balanced preciously in a squat in the tight aisle of a plane.

"Well?" Sarah prompted, wiping the tears away. Her expression had changed, and he couldn't help but understand the sudden blaze of joy and hope reflected in her eyes. "Is that what you came to say?"

"Yeah," he managed to get out. "That's it."

He and Sarah stared at each other, and he knew she heard him perfectly, understood him perfectly, knew him perfectly.

"Damn," the college-aged man in front of them said, turning around. "That's pretty pathetic. You've got to do better than that."

Jonathan glared at the young man briefly, and when he turned back around, Sarah had raised her hands to her face. Her shoulders were shaking. He couldn't tell if she was laughing or crying.

Afraid the annoying student was right and his declaration of love was much lacking, Jonathan burst out, "I love you, Sarah. I'm completely gone on you. I've been crazy about you for ages, but I was too much of an idiot to know it. I've never loved another woman, and I'll never love anyone else. It's always you, Sarah. I'm not good at talking. I never know what to say. You know that. But I'm so sorry I didn't tell you when you needed to know. I was trying to show you. I can't be your boss—not if we're together—but I didn't want you to lose your job. So I had to get funding for the lab and make sure you kept your job. But it was wrong. I was still trying to earn it, when we both know that's not what we're about. I needed to tell you. But please don't leave me. I'll do better. I'll do anything you need from me, anything to make you happy. I need you more than I thought I would need anyone. You're the one who taught me how to love. Please don't cry."

She lowered her hands, nearly sobbing with reaction. He thought—he hoped—it was good.

"Much better," the wife of the couple across the aisle said encouragingly.

"Shh," her husband said. "Don't butt in."

Sarah was still wiping away tears, and Jonathan wanted desperately to reach out for her, to show her how he felt—since he was always so much better at showing than saying. But there was a seat and a woman between Sarah and him, and he could hardly crawl over the woman to get to her.

"I thought you didn't want me," Sarah choked out at last.

"Of course I want you. I'm so sorry I made you believe anything else."

Sarah finally controlled her sobbing, and she just gazed at Jonathan speechlessly.

"Well," the woman between them said, nudging Sarah gently. "Aren't you going to tell him you love him too?"

Sarah's face was almost glowing with emotion that was impossible not to recognize. She didn't have to say anything. Jonathan already knew.

"I'm sorry, sir," a female voice came from above him. "You need to return to the first-class cabin."

Jonathan turned to look up at the flight attendant. "What?"

"It's policy, sir. Passengers aren't allowed into the other cabins. Would you mind returning to your seat?"

"But—" He turned back to Sarah, who was still frozen and speechless.

"I'm sorry, sir. You really do need to go back." He could tell from the woman's posture that she was preparing herself for a crisis.

"But he was just about to propose, I think," the wife of the couple chimed in before her husband shushed her again.

He straightened up to a standing position, looking back at Sarah. She looked beautiful and emotion and bewildered. And cramped in the small seat. "Could I swap seats with her and give her mine in first-class?"

"I don't need your seat, Jonathan," Sarah said, evidently finding her voice. "We can talk when we get to New York."

"Well, I'm not going to sit up there in first-class for hours while you're stuck back here."

"I'm happy to swap seats," the middle-aged woman said, looking thrilled at being part of the situation—or maybe just at the prospect of getting a first-class seat for the rest of the flight. "That way you can sit next to her."

"That would be great," he said, relieved by the solution. He turned to the flight attendant. "Is that all right?"

"Yes, if you both agree. But we really need to get the switch done now. We need to start the food service soon."

So instead of a blissful, romantic conclusion to his declaration of love, Jonathan had to wait while the middle-aged woman gathered all her belongings and got up. Then he had to follow her through the narrow aisle until they reached the first-class cabin. He was almost out of the cabin when he heard Sarah call from back in her seat, "I love you too."

He whirled around, his heart dropping into his gut.

She was standing up, precariously balanced between her seat and the one in front of her. She was beaming at him like the full moon in a dark sky. "I love you too," she said again, so loudly everyone in the cabin could hear her.

When a burst of applause broke out among the other passengers, she looked rather taken aback and self-conscious. She was still smiling though. "I just wanted you to know."

He smiled back at her, hating this flight, this plane, all these people surrounding them, the hours until they got to New York—everything keeping them apart.

He finally got the woman back to his seat, grabbed his stuff, and was able to return to the seat next to Sarah. He collapsed into it, feeling exhausted and unsure what to say and ludicrously happy.

He raised the armrest between them and reached out to pull her against his side, holding her with one arm. She burrowed into him, taking his free hand in hers.

Jonathan was uncomfortably aware of several pairs of eyes on them, surrounding passengers watching them with pleased satisfaction.

"Sorry this all was so public," he murmured. "I always seem to make a mess of things."

"No, you don't."

"Uh, yeah, I do."

"Okay. Maybe this was a little bit of a mess. But I don't mind."

He couldn't stand even the slightest distance between them, so he raised her face to kiss her softly.

When she finally pulled away, she was flushed and couldn't seem to stop smiling. "I thought..." She cleared her throat. "I thought you didn't care enough about me. I mean, I was thinking you did, but then you never said anything, so I assumed you didn't... I couldn't figure out why, if you loved me, you wouldn't say so, so I figured you... you just didn't."

He perfectly understood her babbled explanation. "I know. I'm an idiot and a coward. You know how I am about saying things. I thought I would show you first—get everything fixed up with the lab and then show you how I... how much I... how I feel. I *show* a lot better than I say, and I wanted it to be... I wanted it to be good."

He could only hope she understood his babbling the way he understood hers. From her expression, she evidently did. "You do *show* really well. But I'm sometimes a little insecure. You need to *say* sometimes too. And not just when you feel like you have it all together."

"I know. I know. I'm sorry. I'll do better." He realized the stakes of not speaking when he should have, how close he'd come to losing her. In a rush of feeling, he burst out, "I love you. I love you. I love you."

She laughed and leaned over to kiss him just on the side of his mouth. "I love you too. We'll work on it."

~

They got a hotel in New York after they landed, and they were both so exhausted from the long flight and the overflow of emotion that they just took showers and fell into bed.

But Sarah woke up a few hours later, disoriented and groggy and happy even before she realized why. She rolled over and flopped against Jonathan.

He grunted and reached out for her, obviously still mostly asleep. "Love you," he mumbled, when she nestled against his side.

"You don't have to tell me every minute of the day," she mumbled, although the words made her shiver with pleasure, joy, and excitement.

"Oh. M'kay." His arm tightened around her briefly before he relaxed again.

Feeling a little more awake, she added, "But feel free to say it as much as you want."

"Love you."

She smiled as she stretched out against his big, warm body. "I love you too."

~

Sarah popped a peppermint ball in her mouth, hoping it would give her enough energy to get through another hour of work. She was so tired she could barely keep her eyes open, but Jonathan showed no signs of stopping yet.

She knew how to make him stop. She could tell him she wasn't feeling up to working any more, and he'd immediately tell her to go rest. Or she could make him think about sex, and that was a surefire way to get him to take a break.

But this was the last day before they were going on vacation, and she wanted to finish the project as much as he did.

Maybe one more hour would do it.

He was peering at the DNA strand she'd just pulled up on the monitor, but he turned to her without warning, peering at her with the same focused attention he'd been giving the monitor. "We can stop," he said.

"I don't want to stop."

"That's your fifth peppermint in the past hour."

Her lips parted. "You keep count?"

"You only eat that many when you're ready to drop. You can go to bed if you want. It's really fine."

"I'm not going to leave you here to work all night on your own."

"I'm not tired."

"Yes, you are."

He narrowed his eyes, obviously annoyed at her disagreement.

She reached over and smoothed down the sleeves to his lab coat. "The more tired you get, the more wrinkled your lab coat gets." She felt a sudden wave of affection and wrapped an arm around his waist, stretching up to run her lips across his jaw.

She felt him relax against her, but he murmured, "None of that in the lab. Someone might see."

She giggled. "You know they all know we're together now, right?"

He grunted in affirmation.

"You know they all knew we were going to get together long before we actually did, right?"

He grunted again.

"You know everyone else turned in an hour ago, right?"

As expected, another grunt.

"So why can't I kiss you in the lab?"

There was a smile in his eyes although he was still trying to frown. "Because you distract me. I'm not good at multitasking."

"I know that. I've never seen anyone as single-minded as you. Only one thing can go on in your brain at a time."

His brain had obviously shifted gears, and he pulled her against him, fitting her body against his, which she could feel tightening. "We can go to bed now," he murmured thickly, "if you really want."

She giggled again. "Let's give it another half hour, and then we'll call it quits even if we have no results."

Jonathan wasn't far enough gone in thinking about sex to not be able to pull back, and in another minute he was in full work mode again.

Sarah was not as single-minded. She could think about work with part of her head and also think about how much she adored this man, who was now her partner rather than her boss.

Which is exactly what she did for the next twenty-nine minutes.

～

The next day they flew to Santorini, and Andrew met them at the airport to drive them to Oia to his and Laurel's inn.

Andrew had called Jonathan several times in the three months since the wedding until even Jonathan couldn't deny that he genuinely wanted to connect with his cousin. So they'd agreed to take a long weekend for a vacation and come down to the inn to visit.

Sarah was excited. She'd never been on a romantic vacation with a man in her life. She'd also never been to the Greek islands. Or anywhere in Greece. Or anywhere, really, except the States and Iceland and England for the Damon wedding.

She'd spent most of her life working—just like Jonathan. It wasn't like either of them would suddenly become people of leisure, but still... it was nice to do something for fun every now and then.

She felt a wave of satisfaction as they pulled up in front of the charming, whitewashed inn because Jonathan and Andrew were both laughing at a joke Andrew had just made.

Three months ago, Jonathan hadn't been close to any of his family. But maybe that could change too.

As they got out of the car, they were greeted by three huge German shepherds, who ran over and wriggled wildly until Andrew knelt down to pet them. Grinning, he introduced them to Theo, Circe, and Persephone, obviously proud when they all sat obediently and lifted their paws to shake.

Laurel and an elderly Greek couple had dinner ready, and they ate out on a terrace in the light of a blazing sunset. Even Jonathan seemed relaxed and at ease, telling Andrew and Laurel about their work and asking about the work they'd done on the inn and about Harrison and Marietta, who were living in England now since Harrison worked closely with Cyrus Damon in business.

"What about Ben?" Sarah asked, during a pause in conversation. "Has anyone heard from him?"

"Not a word," Andrew said, his face sobering slightly. "I've tried to call him a couple of times, but he never picks up."

"Maybe you should get a prepaid phone so he wouldn't recognize the number," Sarah suggested.

"He'd just hang up, I think. Harrison said he's e-mailed a few times, and Ben replied once saying he just wants to be left alone." Andrew sighed. "He's not even using his real name. He doesn't want to be a Damon. At all."

"That's too bad," Sarah said, feeling strangely sad. It wasn't like everyone had to be attached to their family to be happy, but clearly whatever Ben was holding onto was eating him alive. "But he made the effort to come to the wedding, so maybe that's a good sign."

"Maybe I should try to call," Jonathan said, frowning thoughtfully out at the water. "Since he walked out because he thought I was getting the cold shoulder."

"Yeah, maybe it would help for him to know that Lord Uncle hasn't cut you off completely, that he's softening in his old age." Andrew winked at Sarah. "Or maybe Sarah should call, since he seemed particularly fond of her."

Jonathan made a guttural noise that sounded almost like a growl, sending the rest of them into peals of laughter.

After dinner, Jonathan said he felt like taking a walk. He seemed to expect Sarah to go with him, and she was happy to oblige.

She really liked Andrew and Laurel, but she didn't want to be around them all the time—not in such a romantic setting.

Jonathan had evidently gotten directions from Andrew since he seemed to know where he was going as they walked down to a pebble beach. It was dark by now, but the moon and stars were incredibly bright, so they had no trouble finding their way.

They didn't talk much on the walk, which wasn't at all unusual. It didn't bother Sarah at all until she started to notice Jonathan getting stiff—the way he only did when he was uncomfortable.

They were standing on the beach, looking out on the water, when she finally asked, "What's the matter?"

He looked at her and opened his mouth, but didn't say anything.

"You have to tell me," she said quietly. She had a flare of nerves. She was so happy, and she was convinced that Jonathan was too. But that didn't mean something bad couldn't still happen. "Is something wrong?"

"No. Nothing's wrong." In the light of the moon, he looked almost sheepish.

She lowered her brow. "So what is it? What are you working yourself up for?"

He gave a low laugh and glanced away. But before she could prompt again he'd turned back. "It might be too soon. I don't know. I'm just no good at this."

"Good at what?"

"At any of this." He gestured between them. "I have no good instincts."

She let out an indignant huff. "Don't you dare say things like that. No one could ask for a better man than I've got. Seriously. You don't have to be a charming talker like Andrew to love someone. I mean it, Jonathan. I feel loved. Really loved with you. You *are* good at it."

He smiled at her and took her face in his hands. "I do love you, Sarah. More than anything. I can't believe you love me back. I still don't understand why."

"You don't have to understand it. You just have to accept it."

"Okay." He paused, but she knew he wasn't finished, so she waited until he continued again. "Anyway, I don't know if it's too soon or not."

"Too soon for what?" She was so focused on easing his concerns that she genuinely, stupidly, had no idea what he was going to say.

Or do.

What he did was stuff his hand into his pocket and pull something out.

She blinked down dumbly at the ring he'd given her for their fake engagement.

"I want it to be real," he said, his voice like gravel. "I want it to… I mean, if you do too."

She was so overwhelmed with surprise and joy and emotion she couldn't do anything but tremble and stare down at the ring.

Evidently, she stared too long. Jonathan stuff the ring back into his pocket. "It's fine if it's too soon. I can wait. I'm not any good at—"

"No!" she cried, grabbing for his hand and, when it came up empty, trying to dig into his pocket for the ring. "It's not too soon. I want it. I want it!"

"Oh." They had a little scuffle until he manage to get the ring back from her. "Well, am I at least allowed to put it on you myself?"

"Right." She was shaking helplessly and had to force herself not to grab the beautiful ring back from him, so much did she want it. "I guess you can do that."

He cleared his throat and picked up her left hand. Then he gently slid the ring onto her finger. He gazed up at her face then, still holding her hand, his expression reflecting everything she needed to know about his love, his commitment, the depths of his generous heart.

A stupid tear slipped out of her eye as she nodded back at him speechlessly.

Then he groaned hoarsely and pulled her into a kiss. A deep one. One that went on for a really long time.

When they finally broke apart, her knees were weak and she had to cling to him to keep her feet.

"That was a proposal," Jonathan said, his arms holding her unshakably. "Just in case it wasn't clear."

She giggled helplessly. "I know it was a proposal, you idiot. And just so you know, I told you yes."

"Yeah, that's what I thought. Just making sure."

There was a kind of joy so deep it couldn't possibly be shaped by words. That was what Sarah was feeling as they walked slowly back toward the inn. She could see on Jonathan's face that he felt exactly the same way.

He held her hand as they walked, and they didn't speak at all.

ABOUT NOELLE ADAMS

Noelle handwrote her first romance novel in a spiral-bound notebook when she was twelve, and she hasn't stopped writing since. She has lived in eight different states and currently resides in Virginia, where she writes full time, reads any book she can get her hands on, and offers tribute to a very spoiled cocker spaniel.

She loves travel, art, history, and ice cream. After spending far too many years of her life in graduate school, she has decided to reorient her priorities and focus on writing contemporary romances. For more information, please check out her website: noelle-adams.com.

Books by Noelle Adams

Eden Manor Series
>One Week with her Rival
>One Week with her (Ex) Stepbrother
>One Week with her Husband

Beaufort Brides Series
>Hired Bride
>Substitute Bride
>Accidental Bride

One Night Novellas

One Hot Night: Three Contemporary Romance Novellas
One Night with her Boss
One Night with her Roommate
One Night with the Best Man

Willow Park Series
Married for Christmas
A Baby for Easter
A Family for Christmas
Reconciled for Easter
Home for Christmas

Heirs of Damon Series
Seducing the Enemy
Playing the Playboy
Engaging the Boss
Stripping the Billionaire

Standalones
A Negotiated Marriage
Listed
Bittersweet
Missing
Revival
Holiday Heat
Salvation
Excavated

Overexposed
Road Tripping

The Protectors Series (co-written with Samantha Chase)
Duty Bound
Honor Bound
Forever Bound
Home Bound

Made in the USA
Columbia, SC
15 February 2019